THE EXORSISTAH

THE

E X O R S

POCKET BOOKS

New York London Toronto Sydney

CLAUDIA MAIR BURNEY

Pocket Books
A Division of Simon & Schuster, Inc.
1230 Avenue of the Americas
New York, NY 10020

First Pocket Books trade paperback edition July 2008

POCKET and colophon are registered trademarks of Simon & Schuster, Inc.

For information about special discounts for bulk purchases, please contact Simon & Schuster Special Sales at 1-800-456-6798 or business@simonandschuster.com

Designed by Jamie Kerner-Scott

Manufactured in the United States of America

10 9 8 7 6 5 4 3 2 1

Library of Congress Cataloging-in-Publication Data

Burney, Claudia Mair
Exorsistan / by Claudia Mair Burney
p. cm
Summary: Seventeen-year-old Emme Vaughn, a homeless girl who can see demons, has a chance to do God's work by assisting a disgraced priest, a nun, and handsome Francis Rivers in performing exorcisms, but must first battle her personal demons, lack of discipline, and teen hormones.
[1. Demonlogy—Fiction. 2. Demoniac possession—Fiction. 3. Exorcism. 4. African Americans—Fiction. 5. Christian life—Fiction. 6. Clergy—Fiction.] I. Title.
PZ7 .B92857Exo 2008
[Fic]—dc22 *2008004564*
ISBN-13: 978-1-4165-6133-0
ISBN-10: 1-4165-6133-1

To Gina Reed

With great love

And these signs shall follow them that believe;
In my name shall they cast out devils.
—Mark 16:17

One

I hate demons.

A dang-gone demon kept me from eating my French fries.

I'd spent the whole day cleaning Kiki's house from top to bottom, and after all that, sat in her kitchen peeling enough potatoes for an army. My black babydoll T-shirt and Apple Bottom jeans sagged on my body like all my diva had forsaken me. My hair hung in knotty, dread-like ropes down my back. I looked a hot mess, but I didn't mind. 'Cause I was gon' have a spiritual experience with my fries.

As I watched them browning to golden perfection I threw my hands in the air and raised the roof just because they smelled so good.

I dipped the spatula in the skillet and turned the fries over, then tapped off the excess oil to a beat as hot and poppin' as the grease. I ain't gon' lie. I did a lil' booty shaking, imagining myself in a pair of supah-bad kick-butt diva boots I saw at Briarwood Mall. Prada. Black and fine as me. Calfskin luxe, with a kitten heel short enough for me to kick some butt in—or run if I had to—and *still* look fly. I couldn't wait for the day when I'd trade my black leather Timberlands for something so fantabulously glamorous.

I was about to put the spatula back into the grease when the hairs on the back of my neck stood at attention. The room chilled in an instant, a twenty-degree temperature drop filling the kitchen with a weighty, suffocating cold. My lungs contracted like I had asthma.

I don't have asthma.

You know how Spider-man has spidey-sense? Well, I've got demon-sense.

I turned around real slow—I wasn't in a hurry to see what had crept into the kitchen. That's when I peeped Kiki's husband, Ray, leaning against the door, leering at me.

Now Ray ain't no joke. Tall, brown, and round in the middle like a teddy bear, only nobody wants to cuddle with him. Not as big as Kiki—who weighed in at 510 pounds—but I didn't want to rumble with him. He'd stuffed his hands inside the pockets of his Dockers. His wide girth strained beneath a white T-shirt. Eyes looked all crazy, and a demon the size of a Hummer trailed behind him.

And all I could think was, *Dang! That's a big'un.*

Now I was used to seeing the freaky lil' demons that always floated around Ray, but this one had to be twelve feet long. Blood-colored with a human-looking face. It had wings extending four feet on either side of its crimson-and-black body. I looked closer and saw the details of an intricate black design covering its back—almost like a beautiful tattoo. Its tail curled like a live wire around its round, paunchy body. I watched it slither past Ray then rush to the ceiling, writhing and baring its yellow fangs like it was trying to smile at me.

Dang! I just wanted to *eat*! I hoped against hope that that thing and Ray would leave a sistah to cook her fries in peace.

Nope.

It wanted to play with me. Shoot, so did Ray. The demon stuck its forked tongue at me, and every time it did, its stank breath pummeled me like a fist.

If you want a good reason not to go to hell, demon funk is a fine choice—well, that and the whole eternal damnation and separation from God thing.

The demon presence wasn't my only problem. Ray kept inching toward me lickin' his lips like he was 'bout to use 'em.

I balled up my fist.

You don't know me like that, Ray.

I may not be able to physically knock a preternatural being upside the head, but I could bust flesh-and-blood Ray in his. Emme don't play no more. I'd had enough of brothas pushing up on me like I asked for it.

And I hadn't had any food!

Ray had better back on up.

All the while, I had to make sure I kept up with the spawn of Satan. I swiped another glance at it and it winked at me, then did a little shimmy with what I supposed was its hips. Finally it zoomed over to hover behind Ray's head.

I hate a show-off, especially a demonic one.

The demon snaked its head out and whispered something in Ray's ear. I didn't think it was asking directions to the nearest herd of pigs, either. Ray must've liked whatever it said. He gave me the once-over. Again. Bared his teeth. Then the demon peeked around Ray's head and called me the "b" word!

Hold up!

Don't *nobody* break on me like that, and for sho' not a punk, useta-be angel.

I rolled my shoulders back, straightened my spine, and stood my full 5'11." The demon turned around, showing the intricate design wrought on its back.

Like a fool I stood there staring at it. The velvety blackness on its back seemed to shimmer. It looked almost animated.

Shoot!

That thing could have incapacitated me as I stood there gaping at it! Mama use to tell me Satan could appear as an angel of light. And I'm falling for that demon trick of trying to distract me from battle.

I put my hand on the black onyx rosary beads my mother gave me before they took her away. She never taught me how to pray with them, but they comforted me anyway. Sometimes, when I touched them, I could hear her voice saying, "Pray for us sinners now, and in the hour of our death."

Shoot. This looked bad for me.

I couldn't do any serious spiritual warfare with Ray tryna molest me. Yeah, I could rebuke the demon, but Ray looked ready to get his swerve on, a very *human* condition.

Clutching the crucifix hanging from my rosary, I felt the same sweet Jesus my mama kissed so many times before she prayed laid out on the cross between my fingers. That's how I put my courage on. If the Lord could hang his broken body on a cross, I could tell a demon in my friend's kitchen to bounce in His name.

I shouted, "I rebuke you in the name of Jesus!" to ol' lusty butt—the demon, that is.

It winced. So did Ray, but neither of them left. Ray stepped closer to me. I knew it was a matter of moments before that man reached out to touch me in a sho' 'nuff dishonoring way. I tried to push him away. Tried to stay calm.

I didn't want to start scrappin' with Kiki's ol' man. Even though Ray had violated a sistah, I wanted to be respectful. But like I said, Emme don't play.

Finally I yanked the crucifix over my head and thrust it toward the demon, which wasn't easy with Ray in my personal space. I'd try one more time before I started whuppin' heads.

"I said, I rebuke you! Get outta here in Jesus' name, or you gon' get your unholy butt beat. Do you hear me? I said, in *Jesus'* name."

Ray laughed in my face. "Girl, that cross ain't gon' do nothin'."

"Jesus will!"

The demon recoiled and slunk away, its red talons drawn up and tail tucked into its wide hide.

Ray acted like I hadn't said a mumbling word.

He backed me up against the stove so dangerously close to the flame beneath the skillet I wondered when I'd catch on fire. Even though the demon had gone, I still needed help.

Think, Emme—like you've got on diva boots.

The hot oil.

I could burn him. It'd be self-defense.

My heart pounded against my rib cage like a convict in jail banging on the bars to escape. I let go of the crucifix.

"The fries are burning. I gotta turn 'em off."

I gotta turn you *off, too,* I thought.

He moved back enough for me to turn around, and I reached

for the knob and twisted it to shut off the gas flame. The grease—still looked hot enough to do some serious damage. I could picture him melting, fries sticking to his seared flesh.

I'm sorry, God. But I can't take no more. I gotta do this.

Gingerly, I grabbed the handle of the skillet with my bare hand. It felt hot, but not so much that I couldn't handle it. Fear gnawed in my gut more than hunger did.

I moved the skillet, maybe a half an inch. Rage stormed inside me. The acrid smell of burnt French fries hung in the air, mingling with the sulfuric stench the demon had left behind.

Ray ran his hand down my arm.

"You betta stop, Ray. Now."

"Why, baby?" he whispered in my ear. "I been thinking about you."

Let's just say that made me burning mad.

Fry him, Emme.

Kiki called from upstairs. "Is something burning, honey?"

I wanted to shout, "Your husband is and will be," but what I yelled was, "Sorry." And I was.

"She'll wait," he said. "Especially for food."

His dis of my girl offended me. "Back up off me before you get hurt." The mix of dread and anger, coiling in me like a snake, created a volatile combination.

An inner dialogue started inside of me. *You'll go to Juvenile Hall if you hurt him, girl.*

They'll have to find me first.

Leave him be, Emme.

Dang. I didn't want to do that.

Ray must have lost patience with me. Grabbing a fistful of my hair, he sneered, "You're a pretty little black thing."

My mind zeroed in on the word *black.* Growing up, the kids use to tease me about my skin color. Said I was so black you couldn't see me at night. Or if I went to a funeral I wouldn't have to put on clothes. Ray's comment churned with theirs, making me even madder.

He slid a hand around my waist. "Come on, let me take care of you," he said.

My mind darted back to the first time he'd said that. I thought he meant something else. Since I never had a daddy, I wanted to believe Ray could be a substitute one. I thought he might be different than the other men, that maybe I'd be safe hiding with him and Kiki until I aged out of the foster system. I had a little more than a month left. Then I could stop hiding, and we'd all be happy.

Dang!

Ray tried to kiss me. For a moment I couldn't move. First of all because Ray's breath was worse than demon funk. But more than that I hated the fact that I'd been in this predicament more times than any sistah should have to be. In foster home after foster home. On the streets. With a lust demon hovering overhead or not.

Ray said, "I'll give you some money."

Like I was a hooker?

"Okay," I said to get him off me. I had my chance. All I had to do was pick up the skillet and stop being a victim.

Only I didn't think the Lord wanted me to fry a brother.

We wrestle not against flesh and blood.

But since flesh and blood touched me inappropriately, I gave Ray something to remember me by: a swift elbow to the neck that left his ol' nasty self hacking and coughing.

I bounced.

The lust demon had, hopefully, gone back to whatever hell it came from, and Ray would no doubt think twice about pushin' up on Emme Vaughn—if I ever saw him again—which I probably wouldn't. Problem solved.

But that left me with my next dilemma. Where the heck was I gon' to go now?

I was officially homeless.

Again.

Dang!

Two

Three o'clock in the morning, and I was standing in the book aisle at Walgreens reading a stupid bestselling book called *The Demon Hunter*. I still looked like the "Queen of the Damned," only not as good as Aaliyah did in the movie by the same name. I doubt she had grease from fries she didn't even get to eat splattered on her clothes.

But Walgreens stayed open twenty-four hours. It gave me an alternative to wandering around Ann Arbor in the middle of the night. Even though *The Demon Hunter*—written by some dude named Hayden Roth—was ridiculous, reading it helped distract me from what went down at Kiki's.

No customers slogged around the store at that hour. Just me. The non-customer. The only other people in the store were two employees: the manager and a squirrelly white dude who seemed like he was too young to work anywhere. Boy cashier looked all of twelve years old, with a shock of dark hair sprouting right out the middle of his head. Harry Potter glasses. Afraid-of-the-dark timid-looking. Took all I had in me not to yell "Boo!" and watch him catapult toward the ceiling. Who hired *him* to work the *midnight* shift? It was beyond me. Not that he actually worked. Real labor might have interfered with his reading time, and I'm not talking enriching, educational reading, either. No, boyfriend stood a few feet away from me with his face buried in the latest issue of the *National Enquirer*.

The manager kept disappearing for long periods of time behind a set of double doors that led to God only knows what or where. Shoot, I just assumed he worked since managers are supposed to do that. Dude's skin suggested he needed a *Bahamavention* or *something* that involved sun, lame recreational activities, and fruity drinks with umbrellas in them.

I could stand a Bahamavention myself, only make my drink *virgin*, 'cause Emme Vaughn imbibed not the fruits of the vine. It's not good for a sistah to have her perception altered. Ever. What happened at Kiki's house was proof enough that somebody would always try to exploit you if they think they can get away with it. Unfortunately, most haters think they can.

Hunger twisted my gut. "That big freak made me burn my fries," replayed in my head like a glitch in a CD, over and over.

I should have grabbed a *National Enquirer*, too. Instead I tormented myself by reading Hayden Roth's new release.

People read this madness everywhere. According to the back of the book the *New York Times* called Roth "America's Scariest Writer." I wanted to call him something, too, and it wasn't "America's Scariest Writer." But I'd have to repent for that, and I had enough to talk to God about as it was. Like where I was gon' live. And why He let ol' trifling, nasty Ray put his hands on me.

I tried to get into the novel, even if it was whack. I could tell by the arrogant tone of the book that Roth hadn't seen any demons for real, because if he had he wouldn't be writing fairy tales.

I wanted to rip that so-called demon hunter book to shreds and tuck its feathery remains behind the romance novels. Fluff up the *love* books. What the world needs now is love sweet love. My mama used to sing that song.

I was mad at Mama, too! Why couldn't she have faked it like I did? Told the people in the hospital what they wanted to hear? We would have a little apartment or something now. And we'd have each other.

I turned my anger back on Roth's book. Sneered at it.

Shoot. Let *me* get a book published. I sho' wouldn't write about demons. I've been seeing the foul things since I was five years old.

But if I *did* write about demons, I'd call it *The Demon Huntress*. I'd *bring it*. My junk would be *live*. The *New York Times* would call ol' Roth "America's *Fakest* Writer."

"Pow, demon!" I said out loud, doing a Karate-chop move with my hand.

Poor *National Enquirer* Boy sucked in his breath and dropped the tabloid, his face even whiter than before—if that was possible.

Guess I startled him. I tried to offer him some reassurance. "I was just daydreaming. It's cool."

He scooped up the *Enquirer* and skittered away like a roach when somebody turns on the lights.

I turned back to the books and magazines, imagining *The Demon Huntress* on the racks with the others. *New York Times* bestselling, fierce action novel with the beautiful protagonist, Emme

Vaughn—diva in kick-butt Prada boots, whuppin' all kinds of devil head.

In Jesus' name!

I kicked one of my black Timbs into the air.

Yeah right. Like homeless high school drop-outs get to be published writers. Dreams seemed pretty useless. I thought of the Langston Hughes poem *Harlem*, the one that starts out, "What happens to a dream deferred?" In the poem, he doesn't answer his own question. I wondered if Langston left the answer to our imaginations so maybe we'd keep dreaming despite our messed-up situations.

If I could make it until Barnes & Noble opened. I could lay my head down on one of the corner tables in the café. I used to go there a lot before I met Kiki. But I didn't go every day so I could stay cool with the management. A few times I woke up to find a steaming mocha and a pastry materialized beside me. I didn't know where it came from, but I'd say a thank-you to God, and to the anonymous angel who fed me.

But I had more than a few hours to kill before the "Big Noble" opened its doors. I felt so tired, I yawned every few minutes, the fatigue wearing on my shoulders like I was rockin' a Baby Phat jacket made out of lead.

Speaking of jackets, I wished I'd thought to grab my jean jacket and purse from Kiki's kitchen chair. I felt like I was freezing. It always took hours for me to warm up after feeling demon cold. Goose bumps still rippled up and down my arms. My stomach growled like a pit bull about to snap somebody in half, too. All of which made Emme Vaughn one miserable sistah.

I fast a lot—sometimes on purpose and sometimes forced—

but this time my empty stomach, heavy heart, and weary body combined to make me a little woozy. I had to eat *something*.

God, you understand I gotta do what I gotta do, right?

I tucked the novel under my arm and let my feet lead me into temptation—also known as the candy aisle.

Just one little candy bar.

Immediately my heart condemned me for even thinking it. And that still, small voice inside spoke up. *Do you want to do that?*

Must've been God talking. I was too hungry for morals. "But you gave Moses manna from heaven. I don't see no free manna bin up in this piece."

Trust Me.

"I'm trying to, but it's easy for You to say. You've got more than a quarter in Your heavenly pockets. It's rough out here, Lord."

Go to the bubble-gum machines.

You'd think God would have known that most of the stuff in those machines cost fifty cents. But I trudged over to the machines, thinking about Kiki. That woman was always singing "Great Is Thy Faithfulness." I wrapped my arms around myself since nobody else was there to hug me.

"If You're so faithful, why am I at Walgreens at three o'clock in the morning, hungry? While Ray's nasty behind is at home asleep in his bed, probably with a belly full of the French fries I peeled?"

I told myself it wasn't right to be mad at God. He didn't force me out of Kiki's house. And I wasn't *really* starving. A whole lot of people didn't eat yesterday, like I did.

What were the lyrics to that song?

Thou faileth not, Thy compassions, they change not.

Something like that. I'd forgotten the words of the song, but I could rail at God for forgetting *me*.

"Where were Your unchanging compassions, or *whatever*, when Ray had me up against the stove? Where were my angels of protection?"

My mama used to read Psalm 91 to me every night before I went to sleep.

"For He shall give His angels charge over thee, to keep thee in all thy ways. They shall bear thee up in their hands, lest thou dash thy foot against a stone. Why didn't it say, 'They shall bear thee up in their hands, lest thy friend's husband take advantage of underaged thee'?"

The bubble-gum machines.

Focus, Emme.

I made it over to the entrance of the store and parked myself in front of the bright red glass and metal dispensers. A bunch of junk: tattoos, stickers, and miniature Disney theme cups—all costing fifty cents—mocked me. One dispenser had tiny plastic aliens for a quarter, but what kind of help could E.T. offer me? I didn't even have a home to phone.

My quarter could get me a rubber friendship bracelet that said BFF, but I didn't have any friends anymore, except for Kiki, and if she were anything like my *legal* foster mothers, she wouldn't have another thing to do with me. One thing I'd learned in my seventeen years was that sistahs will turn on you if their man shoots a move—even if it wasn't your fault. They have a way of making it your fault. And in my experience, if a woman had to choose between her man and me, she'd pick him every time.

Ignoring the useless machines full of stickers, I saw, cowering in the corner, God's ram in the bush for me. It was an ancient-looking dispenser from the Lion's Club offering Red Hots, Chicklets, or peanuts for a quarter.

I had to make a wise choice. The machine looked like it had been there since the sixties, and the peanuts looked about as old as creation. I'd probably break my teeth on those fossils. I'd gobble the Red Hots down too fast, and they'd be gone and I'd still be starving; but the gum had possibilities, and some of my quarter would go to charity to help some kid get new glasses. It'd be my contribution to domestic missions. How could I lose?

Having decided, I put my only quarter in the slot, cranked it, and waited for some of the multicolored squares to tumble into my hands.

Nothing.

Oh no it didn't play me like that!

I put my hand on the top of the machine, trying to keep my hunger-fueled wrath in check, then glanced around to see where *National Enquirer* Boy had gone. Predictably, I spotted him next to the cash register area at the point-of-sales display. I gave the snack dispenser machine a little shake.

More nothing.

A bell sounded, startling me long enough to reconsider destroying public property. I looked toward the main entrance. The sight of the brotha coming through the glass doors made my stomach do a cartwheel, and it had nothing to do with hunger.

Oh Lord, he was *too fine*. I take that back. Brotha man was three, four, *five* fine.

He could have been my ninja twin: dressed in all black, down to his leather Timbs; only he wore a loose-fitting men's T-shirt tucked into his Levi's.

He was a little taller than me, and I wasn't mad at him for that! His baggy jeans hung low, giving a nod to hip-hop chic, but not so low that he'd cause a scandal. A thick leather belt secured them on his hips, which from where I stood, looked as lean and muscular as a Masai warrior's. A black rosary hung down his neck like the masculine version of the one I wore.

My heart went crazy, beating like I'd run a marathon, and my face warmed, flushed from my excitement. My breath came in shallow sips. Usually I wasn't stud'in' these knuckleheads in the streets, but something about this one captivated me.

He'd paused at the entrance when he saw me, and stared with a stunned expression on his face. Recovered, collected himself, and strutted over to the newspaper stand, which happened to be right next to me. He picked up a paper and perused the front page.

I couldn't take my eyes off him, and not because I found somebody checkin' out a copy of the *Ann Arbor News* to be a riveting activity.

His attention didn't waver from the paper which gave me a few moments to absorb his fineness: shiny black curls cut in a low top-fade. Skin the color of cocoa and red clay. Fine-chiseled features with a kinda Latino vibe.

Blacktino! With a hint of sadness around his eyes.

I swallowed hard. The brotha had me counting the days until my eighteenth birthday—exactly thirty-three. I knew Mr. Foxy Brown was no teenager. He wasn't no old-timer . . . looked like maybe he was in his early twenties.

Of course, with the way my day had gone, he'd be like the bubble-gum machine: promising looking, but ultimately disappointing. And cutie might be the kind of man who could take more than twenty-five cents from me.

My stomach howled again, bringing a flash of righteous indignation with the pangs. I gave the Lion's Club machine a hard, swift kick.

Nothing came out, but *National Enquirer* Boy took off running. Cutie looked at me, smirked, and went back to his paper.

I took a deep breath and let out a sigh of resignation. "Okay, fasting it is."

Without my permission my gaze went back to Mr. Fine. I tried to talk myself out of scoping him.

He kept his eyes on the newspaper, but smiled, and man, what did he do that for? One deep dimple stretched a vertical path down his cheek. Then he spoke, and his voice wrapped itself around me like a cashmere pashmina.

"It's not nice to stare, pretty *morena*."

"What makes you think I was staring at you?"

Now he did face me, though he ignored my question. "Shouldn't you be at home in bed?"

See, Emme? All it took was five seconds for him to reveal he's a canine like all the others.

"Dang, *dog*! Can't you ask me my name first?"

He cocked his head and raised an eyebrow. "I take it that when you called me dog, you weren't saying I'm your boy."

"You're a smart puppy, too! Are you housetrained?"

"Take it easy, ma. That wasn't a proposition."

"Tell it to *Dateline NBC*, predator."

"You're the one who was staring. I happen to value my freedom, spicy little *mamacita*. I'm just sayin'. It's a school night, and I'm sure it's past your bedtime. What are you, fifteen? Sixteen?"

His ghetto Spanglish confirmed what I thought about his ethnicity: Blacktino. And fine as he wanna be. But that didn't mean I was gon' answer him.

"And you're *still* tryna get personal information?"

"It's not that."

"It ain't no school night, and I ain't got to be in bed."

The brother laughed at me. "Whateva," he said. "I just don't think you should be hangin' out in the streets alone this time of night, little one."

"*Streets?* Does it look like I'm prowling Washtenaw in stiletto heels and a leather miniskirt? This is Walgreens, hombre. And I ain't little."

"You're little enough, and you're definitely young, *chica*. Too young to be out in the middle of the night alone."

"Maybe I'm not alone."

He gazed at my chest, or so I thought for a second. "I see you're wearing a rosary."

I pointed to the rosary hanging from his own chest. "What's the deal with you? Are you tryna make a fashion statement with *your* rosary?"

"It's not a statement. I use them to pray."

"Well, maybe the One you pray to is with me."

"You must need Him bad, since you're out here assaulting bubble-gum machines."

"It took all my money."

"You must not have very much."

I opened my mouth to say something smart, but he didn't wait for my retort. "I don't think you're really fasting, either. When did you eat last?"

"Yesterday, and I don't need no charity."

"Are you hungry, little girl lost?"

"Naw. And I ain't no little girl."

"You didn't answer my question. You must be hungry."

Before I could respond he sighed and gave me a weary look. "You've got 'runaway' written all over you, ma, and you do look like a little girl lost. Why don't you relax, tryna front like you're all big and grown. . . ."

"I'm almost grown. I'll be eighteen in—"

"What? Two years? Three?"

"Thirty-three days so, you might as well say I'm grown now." I put my hands on my hips for emphasis.

"You ain't grown if you can't vote, ma. You hungry?"

"I said I don't need no charity from you."

"What's wrong with charity? Charity is just love. The Bible says, 'As it is, these remain: faith, hope, and love, the three of them, and the greatest of them is love,' or charity if you're a King James Version sorta girl."

"Maybe I don't want your love, Bible boy."

"God wants you to eat, and He wants me to feed you. So, you wanna eat? Or do you wanna flirt with your hands on your lil' hips, acting like you a woman? Even though I ain't havin' no part of that."

He had the prettiest light brown eyes with tiny, luminous flecks of gold circling his pupils like rings. They mesmerized me and I forgot myself.

"How old are you?" I asked.

"Too old, *chica*." He looked at me, those eyes like two treasure chests brimming with gold, teasing me. "But you are a doll baby, and you've got great taste in clothes. What's that you're reading?"

I glanced at *The Demon Hunter* still in my hand. "Nothin'."

"*The Demon Hunter*, huh? You into stuff like that?"

"I just picked it up. Can't a sistah read?"

"A sistah can read whatever she wants. I like a literary *chica*."

Okay, he was feeling me. And even though he could be a dog, I thought I'd pet him just once.

"You're just saying that because you wanna keep talking. And we're dressed alike. You been following me around, haven't you? Dressing like me so you can get my attention."

"You got my attention because you reminded me of somebody."

"Who would that be? An old girlfriend?"

He ignored my question and fired another one without missing a beat. "What got my attention most is you being out here broke, hungry, and probably exhausted. Which means you don't have anyplace to go. Am I right?"

"You just gon' blow off my question?"

Okay, now I was tryna get information out of him. But only because I couldn't help it. Somebody released a nest of butterflies in my belly, and their wings brushed up against my insides.

For real, I'd never seen such compassion as I did in his eyes, and the kindness in his voice broke through my emotional armor.

"Maybe I got someplace to go. Or maybe . . ."

Shoot.

I'd fooled around and sounded vulnerable. I knew better. In the streets you can't show your tender underbelly. That'll put you in harm's way.

But wasn't he showing me his?

He stared into my eyes and I saw a kind of solidarity. Like

he'd been there, and he was feelin' me—and not in the way Ray tried to.

Okay. I couldn't hang with Mr. Intense gaze. I looked away. Took a step toward the sticker and tattoo dispenser, but he called me that pretty Spanish thing again.

"*Morena*."

His voice resounded in my insides like the first sweet notes of a song he wrote for me alone.

"Look at me," he said.

I did. Had to.

He spoke two words to me—two perfect words: "I know."

I squeezed my eyes shut and shook my head. I could feel my eyes sting, but I didn't want him to see me break down. I willed the traitor tears away.

He repeated, "I know, *chica*."

"What does *chica* mean?"

"God's baby girl. At least that's what it means to me."

I sho' didn't feel like God's baby girl.

I shook it off, but not before he must have seen the shine in my eyes. He didn't make any move to touch me. If he had I may have collapsed into a crying mess in his arms. Or given him a beatdown.

He reached inside his back pocket, pulled out a worn leather wallet, and took out two twenties. He didn't offer the money to me; he set it on top of the Red Hots dispenser.

"There's a Denny's across the street. I'm not going to ask you to get in my car. I hope you're too smart to do anything like that. But I've got a feeling there'll be some old cat in there in a few minutes, wearing all black, who'd be happy to buy you breakfast. All you have to do is go over there."

What the heck?

Any hint of tears disappeared.

I put my hands on my hips again. "Punk! You tryna *pimp* me just because you put forty dollars in front of me? I might be hungry, but I ain't about that."

Shock left him openmouthed for a moment. Then he laughed. "*I'm* the old cat, and all I want is to buy you breakfast. This is a God thing."

When I didn't respond he acted like he thought I'd never heard of God.

"You know? The New Testament? Jesus saying, 'I was hungry and you fed me'?"

"I know what it says."

"I'm tryna feed Jesus through one of his little ones. You look sorta little to me, ma. Okay?"

My stomach answered him with a roar. I clamped my hand over the traitor.

He gave me that dimpled-on-one-side grin again. "I'll take that growl as a yes."

My belly may have said yes, but Emme wasn't so sure. I bit at my lip. I hadn't had the best luck with men tonight, or ever. He seemed sweet, but he was older than me, and my mama said most of the time older meant experienced, and they'd want to experience *me*. I didn't know him, no matter how fine he was or how nice he seemed.

Frustrated, I contemplated my choices. Remain hungry and cautious, or go get a Grand Slam breakfast with the Scripture-quoting hottie?

I didn't exactly mull that one over for long. My stomach wouldn't let me.

And then I smelled something. Sulfur and stank. Demon funk crept into Walgreens.

My gaze flew to the entrance. I didn't see anything around cutie. The bell rang—*ding*—and some character straight out of a Stephen King novel walked in through the entrance doors.

He wasn't outwardly strange. He looked like a regular guy. White, medium height, brown hair. A little chubby. Dressed okay, nothing special or weird. But a hazy, gray cloud hovered around him, giving off evil vibes.

Shoot. That meant one thing. Dude was into something foul, and I wasn't tryna deal with his mess, too.

Let him keep walking, Lord. I'm worn out. And this fine brotha offered me breakfast!

I see crazy clouds around people all the time. Weird-colored auras. People's faces morphing into the shapes of animals. Or worse! Little black men, and I don't mean short brothas. You name it.

I had already fought a big demon. I didn't feel like dealin' with another one. I tried to ignore the man and the evil he brought with him. Did I have to get personally involved every time a whack preternatural being showed itself?

But shoot. It's hard for me to ignore seeing evil. As it was, demon and friend were headed toward the cash register. I didn't know if the hellish thing was gon' influence his human host to rob the store or what. *National Enquirer* Boy couldn't even hang with *me*. He certainly wasn't ready to rumble with a demon.

I fixed my eyes on the pair. The cloud slowly turned as black as smoke from a burning house. Its shape began to shift, unfurling into a human-like form—like a person made of smoke. My heart sank. I knew somebody was about to clown, and the most likely suspect was the dude it came in with.

He'd made it to the cash register. *National Enquirer* Boy materialized. Stuttered a greeting at the man. Now, the manager might have needed a *Bahamavention*, but *National Enquirer* Boy looked like he needed to be raised from the dead. He'd turned white as a ghost.

The familiar burst of adrenaline flooded my body, energizing me for battle with the enemy. I could feel my heart slamming against my chest. Mama didn't give me much, but she gave me Jesus' name, and the Psalms. The Twenty-third came to my aid.

"The Lord is my shepherd I shall not want. He maketh me to lie down in green pastures; he leadeth me beside the still waters. He restoreth my soul. He leadeth me in the path of righteousness for His name's sake."

I had to get ready. Somebody was gonna get a butt-kickin', and I sincerely hoped it wouldn't be me or my new friend.

"Yea, though I walk through the valley of the shadow of death, I will fear no evil: for thou art with me; thy rod and thy staff they comfort me."

I picked up the money cutie had given me and slipped it into my front pocket, too preoccupied to say thanks. I laid the copy of *The Demon Hunter* on top of the dispenser where the money had been. I didn't see squat in that book I could use anyway.

"Thou preparest a table for me in the presence of mine enemies; thou anointeth my head with oil; my cup runneth over."

I crouched to make sure my Timbs were tied tight, took a deep breath, and got up so I could get busy.

"Surely goodness and mercy shall follow me all the days of my life; and I will dwell in the house of the Lord forever."

I rolled my shoulders back. A'ight. Let's roll.

"Lord," I silently prayed, "Can you help me stay feminine-looking? A cute brotha is standing right here, and a sistah still needs to look good, even if she is battling the power of Satan."

Amen.

Now it was time to kick butt.

Three

Cutie's expression had changed to one of dread. His brows furrowed, and his mouth flattened to a frown. For a second I wondered, my heart pounding wildly at the thought of it, if he could see demons, too.

The prospect excited me a little too much. I wouldn't wish that ability on anybody, but the thought of being able to talk to somebody about this . . . if other people could see what I see . . .

I could tell Cutie was experiencing something, so I got right down to business. I looked right in those pretty, gold-flecked eyes of his. "Can you see it, too?"

From the expression on his face I figured my question surprised him. He shot a look in the general direction of the demonic. "Can I see—? What are you talking about?"

I shook my head. "Nothin'. My bad."

My heart crashed down to my empty stomach. Now he was gon' think I was crazy and dip without buying me breakfast.

Dang! That would be the second meal a demon cost me in less than twelve hours. But at least I had the bread the brotha gave me.

Cutie surprised me and took me by the wrist, pulling me behind him. Whatever was going on he thought he needed to protect me. I could totally dig a man willing to put himself between me and a demon.

"You can see it, can't you?" I almost jumped for joy.

He turned around to face me. His gold-dusted eyes bore into mine. He hesitated. Pursed his lips and shook his head. "I can't see anything,"

My smile faded.

He scanned the area, as if he were trying to see, but couldn't. "I can't see it, but I can *feel* it."

Just to be sure . . . "What can you feel?"

"The presence of evil."

I guess he thought about it. He looked even more astounded than when he first saw me. "Can *you* see it?"

"Will I still get breakfast if I say yes?"

"You can get anything you want if you say yes."

I could work with that.

"Oh yeah. I can see it and smell it. It's funky, and not in a good way."

By the look on his face I must've shocked him again, but he didn't spend too much time trippin' on it. I guess he'd gotten preoccupied with feeling evil multiply. Smoky-the-demon shape-shifted again, and took on another physical form less pretty than his previous incarnation.

"Can you still see it?" Cutie asked. "What's it doing?"

"Changing. When it came in here it looked like a gray cloud.

Then it turned into a smoke man. Now, it's starting to look like a big, black worm, and I do mean *big*, with rolls that make me wonder if you cut them, would the thing—you know—grow a new head or tail or something like worms do?"

He crossed himself. Must've visualized it pretty good if the disgusted look on his face was any indicator.

"What else is going on?"

"It's starting to show its face. It's got a bizarre human-looking head, only the face is too long. Like, I don't know, a human-worm-demon-thing would look. And it needs some serious dental work. Makes me wish I had a pair of kick-butt Prada boots with sharp, stiletto heels. I'd use them to kick a hole in its nasty-looking head."

"You can't hurt a demon with high heels."

"Yeah, but a girl can dream."

Poor *National Enquirer* Boy cowered at the cash register. The man must have asked him for help. Kid looked as nervous as the first person to die in a scary movie.

Then the demon let out some kind of weird scream.

I hid behind Cutie a little more. "Awww, shoot! Did you hear that?"

"Hear what?"

The man it came in with started screaming, too. I'd never seen anybody in synchronized screaming with a demon, and yo, it was most unpleasant. But demons do crazy stuff like that, and it can seriously throw you off your game if you're not careful.

Mama said you aren't doing warfare if you're listening to a shrieking between a demon and his evil friend, but she would have if she coulda heard this noise.

I said out loud, "Jesus!" Sometimes, just saying the Name would do.

The man turned. Slowly. All crazy-looking.

Cutie took the rosary off his neck and kissed the crucifix. Looked like he was about to do his own brand of warfare. Since I wanted to know exactly what his brand was, I let him take the lead. But me and Jesus had his back.

Poor *National Enquirer* Boy didn't know what to do with all that demonic energy. He started to shake and cry.

Cutie made the sign of the cross again, with the silver Jesus crucified between his fingers like I hold it. He pointed it in the direction of the demon invoking the Father, Son, and Holy Spirit. Then brought another one of his heavenly friends to the party.

"Saint Michael the Archangel, defend us in battle. Be our protection against the wickedness and snares of the devil. May God rebuke him, we humbly pray; and do thou, O Prince of Heavenly Host, by the Divine Power of God, cast into hell, Satan, and all the evil spirits who roam throughout the world, seeking the ruin of souls. Amen."

I wasn't sure if I should say amen to that, or what. I mean, where I come from you just rebuked a demon in Jesus' name. Maybe you'd ask God to send his ministering angels. But I wasn't used to folks calling on archangels.

He must have done something right. The demon went crazy. It slammed into a display of cheap CD players and telephones. Stuff fell off the shelves. *National Enquirer* Boy screamed like a girl. To him it must have looked like small electronic products were flying around for no good reason. Shoot. I was about to scream like a girl, especially when a pair of headphones flew in my direction like they had Emme radar.

"If stuff is flying that ain't good," Cutie yelled over the commotion. "What can you see?"

"I guess your prayer made him mad—that or the Archangel came and is kickin' his butt. I can't see anything but the demon. Maybe it's throwing some kind of tantrum."

Cutie's unsettled expression let me know this was bad news.

"Why are you pressed? Looks to me like your heavenly friend is doing what you asked him, too."

"Looks to me like we may be dealing with a *devil*, not a demon. And devils are worse than demons."

"That ain't good."

The man with the whatever-it-was—devil or demon—followed its fiendish companion's lead and started slamming himself into stuff, yelling, "I said I want Duracell. The copper-top batteries!" He picked up all kinds of fans, barbecue pits—whatever he could get his hands on—and tossed them around while he shouted obscenities. And then, yo, the big worm thing changed into the smoke man again and jumped right into the man's mouth.

Bro' froze like his Duracell batteries gave out.

It's not like I didn't know people could be possessed. I'd seen demons inside of folks, making them look like wolves or snakes or crazy-looking primates, but as often as I saw crazy stuff like that, I never saw one *go inside* a person. That thing disappeared into him with the ease of the Walgreens manager going behind those double doors.

Almost as quickly, the demon reanimated the man. His body started twisting, and his face grimaced in all kinds of strange expressions. I thought the demon would make him explode, make his organs go flying. And that was gon' make a mess. It seemed I could hear his joints snapping and popping. My knees knocked into each other.

When I could find my voice, I commanded, "In the name of Jesus, come out!"

A low growl came from his throat. His face contorted into another demon's right in front of me—like it was made of rubber or something. This one had a narrow, vulture-like face.

"Jesus!" I said, and I wasn't using the Lord's name in vain.

Cutie shouted, "The Lord rebuke you!"

The man's eyes rolled back to the whites, the growl growing louder.

Man! I couldn't stop staring this time, no matter what my mama once said. Another face of evil emerged, then morphed into a fourth.

I used the best weapon I had again. "In the name of Jesus," flew out of my mouth.

The man seemed to choke on hearing Jesus' name this time. Sound escaped his throat, but since I'd already heard him cussin' and fussin', I knew the spooky guttural voice coming out of him was *not* his own.

"Shut up," it spat at me, then it called me the "n" word *and* the "b" word!

Okay, that was just rude.

He lunged even with those unseeing eyes at me. I wasn't expecting that. All of a sudden we were in a monster flick. And since my new partner was kinda Latino, by default I became the token black person who was gon' die.

But Cutie threw prayers like poison darts at the man, grabbing him before he could get me.

"Soul of Christ, sanctify me; Body of Christ, save me; Blood of Christ, inebriate me; water from the side of Christ, wash me; Passion of Christ, strengthen me; O good Jesus, hear me; within Your wounds hide me; let me never be separated from You."

I wanted Jesus to hide me, too. *Fast.* 'Cause Cutie wasn't holding it down too well. But he kept praying.

"Let me never be separated from You; from the evil one protect me."

That's what *I'm* talkin' 'bout! Protect me, Lord!

The man slowed. He clenched his jaw and growled under his breath. He seemed to lose strength at that part of the prayer. At the same time multiple voices tore out of his throat, uttering the most wretched blasphemies imaginable. It was as if the demons were cussing in surround sound inside of him.

Cutie prayed louder, "At the end of my death, call me, and bid me come to You."

Hold *up*, now. I didn't care for the direction the prayer was taking. I wasn't tryna die up in this piece.

Cutie continued, "That with all Your saints, I may praise You forever and ever. Amen."

Okay, I could deal with that.

"Sho' could use some of those saints right now. Like Samson on one of his good days but yo, no rush to get to heaven, a'ight!"

He didn't have time to commiserate with me about it. The demoniac jerked free and grabbed Cutie by his T-shirt. Threw the brotha in the air and sent him hurtling toward the entrance, but his archangel friend must've been lookin' out. Although he slammed into those big glass doors, they didn't shatter and impale him.

Now the demoniac had me in his grip, calling me out of my name. His racism, misogyny, and hate for all of humanity belted out of his mouth loud and proud. Over and over.

I tried to pull away from the thing, but I hadn't had enough to eat. The effort made me faint and dizzy. "Jesus, help me!" I cried.

Worked when I was little.

Cutie got up and ran toward us praying the Lord's Prayer, while Demon Boy shook me like a Polaroid picture. If Cutie didn't get me out of that man's grip soon, I was gon' black out.

Cutie jumped on the man's back, shouting, "Give us this day our daily bread, and forgive us our trespasses, as we forgive those who trespass against us."

I needed to be forgiven, all right, since it looked like Satan Boy and his foul friend were gon' kill me. I shouldn't have spent most of the day thinking evil thoughts about Ray.

And yo, that demon kept calling me names like it was a gangsta rapper! I didn't appreciate insults! Not even from demons. And I so wasn't feelin' tryna to help his host anymore, which meant I had even more uncharitable thoughts to deal with.

My partner in warfare got to, "And lead us not into temptation, but deliver us from evil."

"Please, Lord," I begged. "Forgive me for all my sins!" Just in case.

I hate demons.

Always making folks act a fool. Including me! Keeping me from eating. Had my thoughts all jacked up. Now one was tryna kill me!

But Cutie bested the man, and he let go of me. I dropped to the floor. He shouted, "Run!" with the possessed man in a headlock.

Run? Not Emme Vaughn. Cutie fought for me. Prayer meeting just got started!

"God, give me strength," I prayed.

Cutie must have been on "auto." He prayed the Lord's Prayer again, the same way, right in the guy's ear.

The demon inside the man appeared to grow weaker. Must have been because Cutie prayed Jesus' words. Anything Jesus said drives them crazy.

The man started writhing and screeching like Cutie was pouring acid on him.

When Cutie got to "deliver us from evil" again, the man let out another blood-chilling scream, and started spinning around in a circle. Fast!

He didn't get dizzy. But Cutie, who was on that crazy ride, did.

I may have been weak and woozy, but I pulled myself up from the floor. "Loose him in the name of Jesus," I said to the demon, even though I must have looked as threatening as a kitten.

He stopped spinning long enough to take note that I'd joined the mayhem again. The demon in him laughed at me!

Emme Vaughn don't like nobody laughing at her.

And another thing. I didn't hear it calling Cutie names, but it called me everything but a child of God.

That ain't right.

Cutie must have gotten a little vertigo. He bolted away from the whirling devil and rested, crouched down, his hands on his knees.

I repeated my command to the demon. "I said loose him in the name of Jesus!"

It cracked up like I was trying out a routine for BET's *Comic View*.

"I *did* loose him," the demonic voice emanating from the man said. It laughed again.

He meant he loosed Cutie.

I had to try that again. Demons have plenty of sense, and obviously I didn't say the magic words. Or I didn't say them the right way. I spoke to it again, careful to tell it to do *exactly* what I wanted it to do. "Leave the store right now, in Jesus' name."

The demon didn't seem to find me compelling enough. He went for my boy again. Since he was still a little dizzy, the demon got him good. Slung him around like a chew toy in a rabid dog's mouth. I needed to do something about that. Something physical like Cutie did for me. I jumped on the possessed guy's back shouting the same old commands at him.

National Enquirer Boy appeared with the manager, who looked less than pleased at us, probably because he had to come out from behind those double doors. He had an ancient security guard with him, The Defender of the Peanuts no doubt, who'd stood watch over the Lion's Club dispenser in another century. Guard Methuselah took out a pair of handcuffs that looked like they had been used to capture slaves and got right in the tangle between us. He had the nerve to clink the cuffs on my boy!

I jumped off demon possessed guy's back and yelled at the security guard.

"You cuffed the wrong person! The one growling, throwing people, and looking like he's gon' star in *The Exorcist: Part Five* is the perp."

My observation seemed to confuse Guard Methuselah, but his hesitation gave me a chance to slam the demoniac guy in the chest, commanding what crawled up in him, "Out! In Jesus' name!"

That sent the security guard off. He meandered like a drunk toward the manager's double doors.

Shoot. If he called the police and they found out who I was, I'd go right back into foster care. I wasn't even tryna to hurt the guy. I wanted to get the demon's attention. And I still had work to do.

I yelled, "Come out, *right now,* in Jesus' name!"

The guy with the demon growled, "I'll be back."

Great. A demon that does Arnold Schwarzenegger impersonations.

Whatever! As long as it came out, 'cause I was the Terminator now.

"In the name of Jesus—"

Before I could finish my prayer the man pushed at my shoulders—with superhuman strength, might I add. He knocked me three feet back, and flat on my behind, then burned rubber gettin' up out of the store.

Guard Methuselah shuffled over to me. "Young lady, I'm going to have to restrain you."

"You can't handle me!" I pointed to my boy. "The only reason you got *him* is because he was busy keeping the demoniac from hurting me."

National Enquirer Boy spoke up in his squirrelly little voice. "Uh . . . sir . . . uh . . . You *did* handcuff the wrong guy . . . uh . . . sir."

Now he tells him! Man!

"Why you ain't say nothing when he did it?"

And of course Roach Boy skedaddled like I was possessed and about to give him a beatdown.

Cutie looked mad, but he didn't let his manners drop. "Can you please get these things off of me now, man?"

I told Methuselah I planned to file a complaint with the district, regional, and national Walgreens managers, call the NAACP, and get Rev. Al Sharpton, Jesse Jackson, and my cousins and 'nem if he didn't free my friend with the quickness.

I had no idea where my cousins were, but I'd find those roughnecks if I needed to!

Guard Methuselah apologized profusely and uncuffed my boy.

Cutie remained cool about it. "That's okay, man."

"No it ain't," I said.

He chuckled. "Yes it is." He looked me over. "Are you hurt?"

"Yeah! And I'm *suing*." But I only had a few scratches and bruises. And a sore butt.

Cutie gestured toward the doors. "Let's get out of here before we end up on the next episode of *COPS*."

"I ain't tryna see the cops, either. I don't want no more drama tonight."

"Amen to that," he said, and like a gentleman ushered me to the door.

Four

Cutie opened the door for me as we exited Walgreens and walked through the darkness to the parking lot. The night seemed more menacing than ever, especially since I knew a possessed man lurked somewhere in the shadows.

Cutie's voice jarred me out of my fears. "Are you sure you're okay, *chica*? Do you think you need some medical help?"

"I don't have any ID on me. And I can't take any chances. What if somebody on the emergency department staff thinks I've been battered—and not by a demon? The first person they gon' look at is you." I tried to stretch a kink out of my neck. "I'm fine," I said, turning my head from side to side. "What I wanna know is what are we gon' do about the possessed man? We can't let him go."

"He's already gone. Hombre is in God's hands now. I'm more concerned about you at the moment. He pushed you pretty hard."

I frowned. "I don't understand why we didn't get the demon, or devil, or whatever it was out of him."

"Some only go out by prayer and fasting. It can take months sometimes."

"I did pray. And fast, too! I might not have fasted on purpose, but I haven't eaten a bite since yesterday morning. And what do you mean months? I ain't never heard of that."

"Don't worry about that now. Our mission is to get you fed."

I meant to say "okay," but instead I started shaking. I looked into his face and saw compassion in him like I saw demons in the possessed man. I wondered if that's what it looked like to be possessed by *God.* By love *Himself.* Cutie's grace touched me, until the bottom dropped. I fell into his arms.

He held me by the waist, and for a second I felt that flurry of butterfly activity in my belly. Then I got a flash of heat and nausea. Hunger slashed through my crushin' on him and chased the butterflies away.

"Ohhhhh," I moaned.

"Hey, are you sure you're all right?"

"My blood sugar must've crashed. I need to eat."

I would have wobbled to the ground, but Cutie's strong arms held me up. I felt like somebody plunged me into U2's "Vertigo" video. On the inside I spun around like that demoniac.

Cutie's voice penetrated my swirling brain. "Hang on, okay, *chica*?"

All I had the strength to do was whisper a prayer. "God, I'm in *Your* hands as much as I'm in his. Please don't let this guy be a sociopath."

I dropped my head on his neck, completely spent.

I had to admit, the brother impressed me. First he put himself between a demon and me and then he carried me to his beat-up, old, gray Camry and tucked me inside. He took me straight to Denny's. He even convinced the people at the restaurant that all I needed was some food. Brotha got a sistah fed fast!

Now I sat in a red vinyl booth, with a Lumberjack Slam breakfast, a tall glass of OJ, and a hottie who knew how to play demon hunter, gentleman, and hero in front of me.

He had coffee.

"Thank you," I said.

But my gratitude didn't quell my anxiety. Talk about showing my underbelly? He could have done anything to me in the state I was in.

But he didn't.

Of course that didn't mean I had to trust him.

Whether or not I trusted Cutie, the least I could do was make conversation. I tried, but every bad thing that had happened to me that night sprang to the forefront of my thoughts and blew out of my mouth. "I was scared when you put me in your car."

"I know, *chica.* I heard your prayer. I'm not a sociopath, okay? I was concerned about putting you in my ride when you were in such a vulnerable position too, but I needed to get you some food. I would have carried you over, but a brotha walking around with a barely conscious young woman might have bought us some unwanted attention. And that would have defeated the purpose."

"You got that right." I speared my pancakes. "For real, though, I'm embarrassed that I let myself get so jacked up."

"You shouldn't be. You were hungry, and all that warfare drained your energy. The Good Samaritan hooked up the brotha he found. I'd have been wrong to leave you laid out on the street."

I wanted to make sure my instincts were right about him. "Why didn't you call an ambulance?"

He paused. Rubbed his finger around the rim of his coffee cup, but he didn't take his eyes off me. "I thought about doing that at first, but I know what it's like to be that hungry. And some of the things you said made me think you didn't want authorities on to you."

I expected him to ask me what I was hiding from, but he didn't. *Interesting.* I decided to grill him some more. Maybe he really did know what I was going through. From experience.

"When you said 'I know' to me at the bubble-gum machine, you weren't playing around, were you?"

"Nope. I don't play around."

"How do you know I'm not a criminal?"

"Demon's ain't all I can feel."

"You bought me breakfast. Gave me forty duckets. Do you always spread the love like that?"

"I wouldn't necessarily call the money I've invested in you a lot of paper."

"So you pass out bread like that to anyone who needs it?"

"I try to be generous, but no, most people don't get that much from me. I might give 'em some change or a couple of bucks. But . . . I don't know . . . it's like I said. You remind me of somebody."

"Who?"

He didn't answer me.

Jealousy sliced through me. I tried to ignore it. "She must have been the bomb."

Again, he left whoever she was to my imagination, but I wanted him to keep talking. How else could I figure him out?

I ventured another question. "What do you do? Why are you out at three o'clock in the morning? You a Scripture-quoting drug dealer?"

"It's Friday night. People do go out at night who aren't tryna sell dope."

"The clubs close at two A.M."

"But musicians aren't finished breaking down at two. And sometimes they have to talk to people after the show. I'm in a band. I'm almost always out late on the weekends."

Okay, him being a musician was hot. But I needed to contain my enthusiasm.

He leaned forward, moving his coffee cup aside. "Do you know what three A.M. is?"

"No."

"It's called the witching hour. It's the reverse of the holy hour—three P.M.—when Jesus died on the cross. Demon activity is strong at this time of night. When I saw you standing there gazing with longing at the bubble-gum machine—that is, before you started checkin' *me* out—I was worried about you. The witching hour is not the time for one of Jesus' little lambs to be out and about, hungry."

True dat. I'd had enough demons attack me around that time to know it was so.

He went on. "The night is full of predators."

"The night is full of more than that."

"That's right. It's full of demons and their charges, along with the normal zoo full of hustlers, pimps, and wannabes who will see a pretty little *morena* like you and pick up on that hunger you got goin' in your belly. You could have done worse than have a Good Samaritan stumble upon you."

"I know that, a'ight? I said thank you. I'm grateful."

"So what's the next step gonna be?"

"What do you mean?"

"Where do you plan to go after you leave here?" He took a long drag on his coffee, set the cup down without taking his eyes off me.

I shrugged. "I'm not sure where I'll go. Maybe I'll stay here for a few hours, if I can. Barnes and Noble opens at nine."

"If you remembered the story of the Good Samaritan, part of the hook-up was to take him somewhere to heal his wounds."

"I didn't get hurt that badly."

"More ways than one way to be wounded."

"You don't even know my name. How do you know if I'm wounded or not?"

"Wounded girls don't have anyplace to go. They're the ones who faint from hunger and who are more afraid than they let on. They think a bunch of slang will make them look tough, not realizing they can speak like their intelligent selves, and still be perceived as strong."

"I am being myself. I slip with the Ebonics when I'm mad."

He didn't argue with me. Just went back to his spiel. "I've met a few wounded sistahs in my day."

"Like the one I remind you of?"

His expression turned serious. "She wasn't a girl. She was a *woman.*"

"Oh, it's like that?"

"What's your name, wounded girl?"

Might as well chill and stop pressing him about the mystery

sistah. Now that he'd called her a *woman*, I didn't think I'd like his answer.

"My name is Emme Vaughn."

"Emma?"

"No. Em-*me*. It sounds like the television award, Emmy, only I spell it with the letter 'e' at the end instead of 'y.'"

"Em-*me*." He nodded like he liked the sound of that.

I thought of how content I could be, just being quiet and staring at him. His exotic Afro-Latino looks compelled me. His black curls glistened, even in the harsh fluorescent lighting, and that skin, all earth and clay–looking, made me want to reach out and touch him.

But I ain't touchy-feely.

The set of his jaw was a little stern. It begged to be soothed, but his eyes? Nothin' hard about 'em. I saw light—the God kind—in his warm, welcoming eyes, and not because they had gold flecks in them.

"What your name?" I asked.

"Call me Frank."

"*Call* you Frank? Is Frank some kinda moniker or something?"

"Maybe that's my name, Emme Vaughn."

"Or maybe you're lying, brotha Frank's-not-your-real-name."

He drummed his fingers on the table for a few moments. "Why don't you finish your breakfast?"

I took a bite to humor him.

He slouched back against the red vinyl of the booth. "You can call me Frankie if you don't like Frank. I don't like it so much now that I'm older, but you can call me that."

"And how old *are* you anyway?"

"I'm old enough to know better than do whatever madness you *think* I might be up to. How old are you, Emme Vaughn?"

"I told you my age."

"Sixteen?"

"That ain't what I said."

"Oh, you're fifteen."

"I didn't say that, either."

We could go round all night. I didn't want to admit it, but I might have met my match in him. I gave in. A little. "I'll be eighteen in thirty-three days."

"But you're not eighteen tonight, are you, ma? You're a minor. And I'm not. I want to help you out, Emme. Feed you. I was hoping, if you felt like it, maybe you could tell me about that . . . you know . . . that thing you do."

"What thing is that?"

He glanced around the restaurant. Lowered his voice. "You see demons."

It tickled me how he said it. Made me want to tease him. "So, you think I'm like that little boy in the movie *The Sixth Sense,* only I whisper, 'I see demons.'"

He tilted his head toward me and gave me a sly smile. "Some people believe seeing dead people *is* seeing demons."

"Others believe that souls of the dead can possess people, too."

"You got experience with that, Emme?"

"This time I'm the one who's not gonna answer."

"Come on, Emme. Show a brotha a little love. I want to know what it's like. You gotta admit that's a heckuva skill."

"Maybe I don't like showing love to people whose name I don't know."

Laughter spilled out of his mouth and caught me by the heart. Good laughter, without a hint of anything sinister. I let the sound of it wash over me in waves of something that felt like joy.

Oh, Lord. Is he as all right as he seems?

He shook his finger at me. "Ah, ah, ah. Me no tell, but nice try."

"What kind of Latino name do people diminish to Frank?"

"You're as persistent as a pit bull, Emme Vaughn. I told you, girl, call me Frank. Or Frankie. Do you prefer Frankie? You seem like you'll be one of my Frankie people."

"How many Frankie people do you have?"

"A few. And they're all special."

"Females, all of 'em. Right?"

Again, his laughter tickled my heart, leaving its fingerprints.

"You ever been to jail, Frankie-is-not-your-name-either?"

His eyes widened, and he twisted his lips into a smirk. "Jail? Wait, I thought we were 'sposed to be talking about you."

"What did you do?"

"Do I look like a thug to you?"

"I don't think there's one look for thugs. And I ask because you mentioned avoiding the police."

"You wanted to avoid them, too. That's wisdom in some cases."

He leaned back against the vinyl and crossed his arms, but kept his eyes on me, with that smirk on his face. I'd asked him several ways and still hadn't gotten an answer. So once again, I posed the question. Differently. "Were you falsely accused of something like all brothas say they are, and had to go on lock-down?"

"No, I was not falsely accused of something and had to go on lockdown." He really had a laugh about that answer.

"So you really did something?"

"Are you done, Emme Vaughn? Eating, that is."

"Oh, I'm done all right."

"I'd like for us to pray together and give thanks. We were in too much of a rush to get food into you before. Do you mind?"

I shook my head. Way to get off the subject.

He reached for my hand and grasped it. Something akin to electricity jolted me.

Aw, man!

I felt fireworks, and something more—something different. It was as if we made some kind of *soul connection* that went as deep and wide as one of the Great Lakes. Heart deep. Maybe even deeper than soul deep—*spirit* deep. It was like I could *feel* him in my secret place—the place reserved for God only. How did this brotha get all up in my secret place of the Most High?

And somehow I was transported into that same place inside of *him*—like I was walking around inside his heart of hearts, and it was a good place to be.

Yet I still heard every word of him thanking God.

"We give You thanks, Almighty God, for all Your benefits. And may the souls of the faithful departed through the mercy of God rest in peace. Amen." He released my hand, and I opened my eyes to find him staring at me.

"You got inside of me," he said.

"What?"

"I saw and felt you in my . . . I don't know, *chica.* It was like you were in my soul, as clearly as I'm sitting here."

"Bro', you're trippin'."

"I'm not, and you know it. It was weird, but when I touched your hand and we prayed, it was like I could see you without having my eyes open. You were praying with me, but you were thinking about how you could feel *me.* And *you* were trippin' on it. But I watched you. I saw and felt all of it."

His head went down like he was searching for what was happening and the Formica might have the answer. "All right. This is too crazy, we need to—"

"Francis?"

His head shot up. "What did you call me?"

"That's your real name."

He blinked, looking astonished. He buried his face in his hands, as if that would erase his confusion. Looked back at me. "This has never happened to me before, and believe me, I've experienced some tripped-out things. How did you discern my real name?"

"I could feel . . . I don't know . . . some warm, peaceful feeling, and then there it was. I just knew it."

His fingers drummed the tabletop with excitement. "That's amazing. I don't tell anybody my real name. It ain't even on my ID."

Whatever we'd experienced had a lingering effect that went beyond our physical touching, and although it wasn't as powerful as when we were praying together, I could still feel his mind racing. One thought stumbled on the heels of another, ideas tripping and falling inside.

He shook his head. I could feel something nagging at him—something about me, but I couldn't quite reach it now. I wondered if I could find what troubled him if I touched him again.

"Just say it."

"Say what?"

"What's bothering you."

His face turned serious. He bought a little time splaying his fingers out on the tabletop and watching his hands. Finally he said, "Okay, I will. I saw you fasting. Too much. You'll get sick if you don't eat more than one meager meal a day."

My head snapped up, "You know I do that, too?"

"Besides the fact that you are thin enough to be a runway model, yeah, I saw it."

Suddenly I didn't like this thing. "I'm feeling a little exposed."

"Exposed? You're the one divinely takin' names. Nobody called me Francis but my mother. I can guarantee you that."

Apparently he was as wide open as me.

"How much could you see about me?" I asked.

"Not everything. Some things were crystal clear, but other stuff was hazy. Sorta like bad reception on a television."

"That's exactly what seeing demons is like! Sometimes I can see a demon like I'm looking at you, but I might only see one when there are dozens nearby. Or angels. There can be a legion of angels, and I'll only see a few."

"Dang, girl! You can see angels, too?"

"And people."

He tilted his body toward me, excitement bursting out with his flurry of questions. "What kind of people? Like ghosts? Or saints?"

"Like how Jesus saw Moses and Elijah when He was praying."

"You pray like that?" He looked like he was about to fall over. "With so much piety that the prophets come and kick it with you?"

"Naw, boy! What I see isn't based on performance or anything. At least I don't think it is. If I had to depend on my works I ain't seeing nothin'!"

"Who have you seen? And tell me what angels look like. Do you get scared when they show themselves? Do they speak to you? This is crazy!"

My hackles went up. "It's not crazy! No crazier than us seeing and feeling each other's thoughts because we prayed together. I'm as sane as you are, and I don't do this junk on purpose. It just happens."

"Whoa, Emme. I didn't mean it like that."

"What did you mean? Crazy is crazy, isn't it?"

"I meant I've never met anybody with those kinds of charisms. I'm amazed, that's all."

"Charisms?"

"Gifts. From the Holy Spirit."

"You don't know what you're talking about."

He watched me like he thought I'd sprout another head. Thank God the waitress showed up, an energetic sistah with a ponytail weave that bounced whenever she did. She asked if she could take my food away and refill his coffee.

"Yes, please," we said at the same time.

The synchronicity between us unnerved me. Like he could still read my mind.

When the waitress left he asked, "Has what happened between us happened to you before? Like somebody else touched you, and they got your gift and you got theirs?"

"What I got ain't no gift. And no, it's never happened to me before." Since I didn't like where this was going, I flipped it. "What about what you? I could *feel* stuff all of a sudden. Tell me about your gift."

He shrugged it off. "It's nothing, really. I *feel* things. When that man with the demon came into Walgreens the whole energy in the store changed; like, an oppressive, heavy vibe came in and drained all the peace and love out the store. And I feel other things. Sometimes I can feel people's suffering. I feel their story. And they're always sad stories. You know? The feeling feeds me information. It's hard to explain."

"You don't have to explain it now. I think I'd rather *see* stuff than *feel* it."

"Why is that, Emme?"

"Feeling is too hard." I stared at crumbs on the table that had escaped my Lumberjack Slam.

"You've been hurt a lot. I saw the men who . . . hurt you."

My head shot up. "I don't wanna talk about it. A'ight?"

He nodded. "It's cool. If it makes you feel better I didn't get digital movies and surround sound. Mostly I saw *you.* The vulnerable you who is intelligent and strong and could use a few breaks. I like what I see."

I raised an eyebrow at him. He blushed.

"I didn't mean that the way it sounded."

"Yes you did."

"Then I shouldn't have meant it like that."

For an uncomfortable few moments neither of us spoke. He looked toward the kitchen rather than at me. I suppose he needed to break the power of whatever was weaving the two of us so tightly together.

"You go up in your head when you feel like things are getting to be too much for you, don't you, Francis?"

"Tell me more about seeing," he said, ignoring my question again. "What's going on when it's all weird and hazy?"

"Heck if I know. All I can tell you is that when it's not clear I see clouds, light, colors, shadows. But sometimes I don't see anything. And I can't adjust the focus at will. Sometimes the veil lifts, and whatever separates us from the spirit world is moved to the side for a moment. But God won't let me see everything. Maybe I couldn't deal with it. All I know is one moment I see, and the next I got on a pair of *Men in Black* Ray-Bans. And I see through those glasses darkly. You know?"

"I do now," he said.

Francis's expression turned earnest. I knew he was about to ask for something. He didn't disappoint me. "Something is happening between us, some kind of God thing. I want to know more about you, Emme."

He was cute, but I didn't know if I wanted that. But man, when I looked into those eyes . . .

Now would have been a good time for God to say something to me. But He wasn't tryna holla right now. I compensated by tryna gather enough information to make an informed decision. "You say you're not a minor. But that could mean you're only eighteen. How old are you? No evasion, okay? I'm losing patience with this little dance."

"I'm twenty-one."

"And when did you turn twenty-one?"

"A few days ago."

He wasn't too old for me.

He sipped his coffee. Watched me a lot. Made beats on the table, and I could tell he had mad rhythm skills. I guess he was gathering his courage. He got down to business. "I'd like to keep talking to you, Emme. I mean that sincerely."

"We can sit here as long as you'd like. You keep buying the coffee, and I'll keep talking."

"I'm ready to go. It's been a long night."

I glared at him. His gaze shifted to his hands, as if my scrutiny embarrassed him. Or was he ashamed that he couldn't hide his interest in wanting more from me, despite his trippin' about my age?

I asked him point blank, "What do you have in mind? And you'd better be straight with me."

"Are you always this difficult?"

I searched his face for any hint of something unsavory. I didn't see anything, but didn't know if it was because he was so fine and a part of me was diggin' him, or not. "It's almost four now. I'm tired. You must be tired. W'sup?"

He blurted out, "I know a place you can go that's safe."

"I'm listening."

"You just have to come home with me."

I rolled my eyes toward heaven. "Wanna speak up now, God?" I prayed aloud.

Five

God didn't say jack to me.

I sat in that booth, posture rigid, arms crossed, with my gaze roaming to and fro, checkin' out everything and everybody but Francis.

I listened to the quiet chatter of the few patrons, and the droning voices of the staff pouring out of the kitchen. Some whack-sounding smooth jazz played in the background.

I had to count the cost here. Okay, he had treated me like he was a Good Samaritan in every way, and maybe he was finishing the job. In the story, the Samaritan did take his boy to a safe place.

Then again, every pimp I've ever met—and I've met a few—played the same game. They be all nice, treating you like a straight-up princess, and the next thing you know you're spending time with their "friends" and you don't have to do nothin'. Until you *do*.

Not Emme Vaughn.

Wouldn't have been hard for him to read me this time. My face said it all.

He leaned over the table. "It's the home of a priest. He's been known to take a troubled teenager in before."

"A priest?"

"He's an old man, Emme. And he's terminally ill. And a woman—a nun—is staying there to take care of him. And she don't take no stuff from anybody. Nobody's gonna do anything they aren't supposed to in that house. I promise."

"And where is this place?"

"It's in Inkster."

"Inkster! I ain't going to Inkster!"

"Ain't nothin' wrong with Inktown. It's full of good people."

"I grew up in Inkster. I know all about it. I've got plenty of bad memories from the projects, bro', and I left a few people behind I ain't tryna see." I didn't tell him that, on the other hand, there were a few who would be good to see, and I'd be tempted to risk whatever freedom I had going to see them. But those I wanted to avoid . . .

Naw. I couldn't do Inkster.

Or was the street the bigger risk?

He asked, "Is somebody after you?"

I played his game and ignored the question.

He gave up after a long pause. "Emme, nobody's gonna turn you in to foster care thirty-three days before your birthday. Not where I'd take you."

"How did you know—"

"I know a lot, Emme. And it didn't take some shared spiritual charism for me to figure that out."

"People say they're gonna help, and they end up . . ." I thought about Ray. "*Not* helping."

"You have my word, Emme."

"Your word don't mean nothing to me."

"It means something to me."

"Why do you live with a priest and a nun?"

A sheepish expression crossed his face. "I just do. And I didn't want it to sound like I'm a dog, asking you to come home with me."

"But you are asking me to come home with you, clown!"

"But not like a dog," he said.

I forced the air out of my lungs. I couldn't buy his story. Why would he live with clergy? "I knew you were too good to be true. You told me that crack lie 'cause you think it'd be that easy. Man. Are *all* men animals?"

"I said I live with a priest and a nun! What sorta crack lie is that? Not that I smoke crack or tell lies."

"I've heard all kinds. You wouldn't make a good pimp. You ain't even a good mack."

"I don't have any pimp or mack aspirations, so I'm cool with that. I'm telling you the truth, Emme. I can prove it without you even having to get in my car again."

"How?"

"Let me make a call. And if you're not convinced, pray about it. But I think God will give you a yes. You can trust me, Emme. What other options do you have? All you've got is forty dollars. How long is that gonna last?"

He was right. And no other bright ideas were falling out of the sky. This time I sighed. "Make your call."

Once again I wished I could see the future instead of demons.

He pulled out his cell phone. Dialed a number, put the phone to his ear, and waited.

Voice mail must have kicked in. He hung up, and dialed again. Repeated the process two or three times until he got an answer. I watched him like a pot of grits cookin'.

He looked perfectly calm. "Hello, Mother Nicole? I'm sorry to call so late, but I want you to talk to someone. She's important to me."

He waited and listened to what she had to say. Then he blushed and showed me that dimple again, and his grin made me soften toward him and whatever whack conversation he wanted me to have with whoever was on the line.

He *did* call her Mother Nicole, but what if that was some kind of hint so she'd play along?

He handed me the phone as if it were a peace offering. "I know you're salty with me," he said, "but I'm not trying to trick you. I didn't want to say much to Mother Nicole so you wouldn't think I was setting the conversation up. You can ask her whatever questions you want. Go ahead. Take the phone."

I took his phone and held it to my ear. It retained the faint scent of whatever cologne he wore. "Hello."

The voice on the other end greeted me with a hearty, "Hey there."

I could tell two things right away: She was white and older than him. Not that her voice sounded like a little old lady's, but she had a kind of authoritative voice, like she'd lived through a lot, in years and experience, and didn't take no stuff.

I cleared my throat. I felt kinda stupid talking to a strange white lady on somebody else's cell phone at, like, four o'clock in the morning, but what else was I gon' do?

"W'sup?" I said into his cell that smelled sweet and musky like his cologne. "Is your name Mother Nicole for real?"

"It's *really* Mother Nikolai, but nobody spells or says it right, so yes. I am Mother Nicole."

"Francis tryna take me home."

She sucked in her breath, then dramatically exhaled. "Oh my! He lets you call him Francis. You must be very special, indeed!"

"Not really. Check this out: I told him I don't know him like that. He said you would vouch for him or something." I added for kicks, "You're not really his girlfriend, are you?"

She cackled into the phone. "Lord, have mercy! Frankie must be laughing his head off now."

"Naw. He ain't laughin'. And he heard me ask you. He gay?"

"Heavens no!"

"Is a girl who's, like, almost eighteen too young for him?"

"I don't think so. Of course, that depends on the girl."

I winked at Francis. "I know, right? Tell me about this place where y'all live."

"It's the house Father Miguel lives in. I don't know how much Frankie told you, but I'm here for Father Miguel's hospice care. The house belongs to All Souls Catholic Church, and Frankie has been staying here for three years, but he can't take care of Miguel all the time. He really needs a nurse at this point."

"Why he staying with a priest?"

"You'll have to ask him that yourself, lovie."

"Is this on the up-and-up?"

"It's as straightforward as they come."

"How many teenagers has this priest dude taken in?"

"Just Frankie. And he'll take you if you come."

"I haven't decided yet. Is he a freaky molester priest?"

She sighed. "He does not molest people. Let me ask you a question. Why does Frankie want to bring you home?"

"I don't know. He said he wants to talk more."

"That must be some conversation, because he's never brought anyone home."

"He said something about being a Good Samaritan and me needing wounds healed."

"He's a good judge of the walking wounded. Why don't you come? See what happens."

"Am I gonna be safe if I ride with him?"

"I'd trust my godson with my life," she said. "And I don't trust just anybody."

"For real?"

"Absolutely."

I said a quick, silent prayer asking God if it was cool to go.

Francis must have been happy. God gave me His yes.

Six

We got back to the Camry, and he opened the door for me and waited while I got myself straight. As soon as I put my seat belt on, I closed my eyes to rest them and promptly fell asleep.

I woke up to the feel of Francis's hand moving my hair off my face and his voice whispering my name. I rubbed at my eyes, trying to wake. When I opened them I saw his peering at me. I sho' could stand waking up and seeing him every day.

"Did I sleep the whole way here?"

"Yeah, it's okay." He gave my hair one last stroke. "I like your hair. It's so long and beautiful. Are you tryna dread?"

I jerked myself up. "Naw, I ain't tryna dread!" My hand went defensively to my unintentionally budding locks. "My hair is a hot mess. Kiki was supposed to put it in cornrows before—"

Don't go there, Emme.

I tried to calm down. "So, we're not in Kansas anymore, huh?"

"Nope. Welcome home, Emme."

We'd parked in front of a little bungalow house right next to a church, just like Mother Nicole said. I turned my gaze toward the house of God. "That must be All Souls. Cool name, by the way."

"Don't let the name fool you. Father Miguel isn't as accepting as his parish's name suggests."

"So, you're Catholic?"

"Not yet. But you could say right now I'm being initiated into that particular body. I'm still working through some . . . issues. What about you?"

"I went to Pentecostal churches most of my life. My mama had this rosary, though. Never did teach me how to use it." I fingered the black beads around my neck. "She told me these can protect you from demons."

Not that it had protected Mama.

"Dang. We so aren't gon' work," I teased. "My mama said Catholics and Protestants don't mix."

"I'm not Catholic yet."

He laughed when I startled, like *National Enquirer* Boy, at his comment. But he turned serious fast. "My father says the same thing, but most of the time I think he's talking about me and him. My mother was Catholic, but wouldn't let me have anything to do with the Roman Church. She raised me a Protestant."

"She must have had a serious beef with the Church."

"Yeah. I'm sure that beef was my father."

"What about him?"

"He broke her heart."

"Did he break yours, too?"

"Does it all the time."

Then *blam!* An invisible fifty-foot wall shot up between us. End of conversation. I was tired anyway. I stretched out my arms and legs, then folded back into myself.

"I feel so sleepy I could stay right here in the car. But not in Inkster. When I lived here, those projects across the church's parking lot were a war zone. Ain't no way I'm sleepin' in the ride, not even if your church was inside this Camry."

"Girl, the projects better watch out for Emme Vaughn."

"You think?"

"I know. But it's okay to be vulnerable sometimes, as long as you're strong when it counts."

Shadows from the night covered his face, but I could still see how pretty he was. "I guess it must always count. Because I don't seem to get too many breaks to be vulnerable."

"I know what that's like. You ever read *The Message*?"

"Yeah!" I beamed. "I'm totally down with *The Message*."

He gave me a sly, one-dimpled smile. "Don't let Father Miguel hear you say that. He'll brand you a heretic like he's pretty much branded me."

He got up from his reclining position and grabbed the black leather book from the backseat. His well-worn copy showed me it was a favored friend of his.

I felt a little sorrow in that moment, and for the life of me, I couldn't tell whether it was his or mine.

Francis righted himself in the driver's seat. "Have you read Matthew 11:28 in here? I love it in this version."

I had read it, but you can't have too much Matthew 11:28 from *The Message*.

He scooted around and sat with his back against the driver's door, his knees pointing toward me. Francis read aloud. "Are you tired? Worn out? Burned out on religion? Come to me. Get away with me and you'll recover your life. I'll show you how to take a real rest. Walk with me and work with me—watch how I do it. Learn the unforced rhythms of grace. I won't lay anything heavy or ill-fitting on you. Keep company with me and you'll learn to live freely and lightly."

"Nothing heavy or ill-fitting, huh? Sounds like some Jesus couture. I love it. Sign me up for that."

"Looks like you're already signed up the way you whip on a demon."

He turned his head and gazed out the driver's-side window into the night, sighed, and rested his head against the window. "I know things feel heavy sometimes." He turned back to me. "It'll be daylight soon. Mother Nicole is waiting up for us."

I got suspicious again. "What did you do wrong?"

"Didn't we already have this discussion?"

"You said these people would protect me. They must be doing the same for you. Why do you need sanctuary with a priest?"

"I don't have sanctuary with him. And maybe it was somebody else who did something wrong."

"Who would that be?"

For a moment his eyes darkened to almost amber. But he got his cool back quickly. "I live here because I didn't have anyplace to go and . . . somebody . . . told me about him. It's an arrangement Father Miguel and I are cool with. Most of the time."

He added metal spikes to that fifty-foot wall he'd erected, threw in a water-filled moat, complete with crocodiles and a big sign that said "Back Off." I didn't even try to break through.

"You gon' take me in now and keep me safe from da hood, or what?"

"Yeah, we're going in, but it's not the projects I'm worried about you running away from."

"Meaning?"

"We'll get to that soon enough."

~

The house looked older than the projects across the parking lot. If its sturdy, determined air were any indicator, it would still be around when those joints got torn down.

Mother Nicole greeted us at the door in her full nun regalia. She had her hands on her wide hips and started in on Francis as soon as we stepped inside. "I thought you'd never get out of that car. You do realize I have the morning office in fifteen minutes?"

"I know, Mother. I'm sorry."

She ceased her scolding to gather him into a hug. "You good little Samaritan. And what a pretty one she is."

Francis blushed.

She let go of him, and looked me up and down. "You're tall, but tiny. We definitely have to fatten you up."

Francis tried to be helpful. "She fasts like an ascetic."

The hands went back on Mother Nicole's hips. She scowled at me, but her eyes were like two hazel stars, twinkling. "Do you think you're up for sainthood or something? You're still a growing girl." She patted both her hips. "So am I, but for different reasons."

Kiki always cracked on herself about her weight. A wave of sorrow hit me. *I'm never gonna see Kiki again.*

Mother Nicole said, "Follow me, lovie."

I tracked behind her. She led me through a pristine-clean, comfy-looking kitchen area and into the living room, Francis right behind us. All the furniture looked old—nothing too fancy, but nothing shabby, either. A nice house. Like a grandma's house. Mother Nicole's welcoming presence made me almost feel like I could chill for a minute.

"Make yourself at home, lovie," she said, "I know you're tired, but I want to visit a bit before you go to bed."

Dog tired, I plopped onto a cushy upholstered wing-back chair. I liked her so much I didn't mind staying awake a few minutes more. I still kept my guard up. A little. Francis lounged on the sofa, his back against the armrests, ankles crossed, shoeless feet on the cushions.

Mother Nicole sat in a comfy-looking reclining chair across from where I sat. Someone had casually draped a crocheted afghan across it. [When she asked me my name, I realized I'd never told her.]

"It's Emme, like the television award, except there's an 'e' on the end instead of a 'y.'" I felt kinda nervous, rambling, "My whole name is Emme Kate Vaughn. I was named after my grandma. I never met another Emme, but I heard there was this plus-sized model with my same name. I mean, not the Kate Vaughn part. The Emme part." I stopped myself. I was starting to sound crazy, and that was the last thing I wanted her to think.

She regarded me with a look of kindness. "Emme Kate Vaughn is a pretty name for a very pretty girl. I see so many LaKweshas and Shaniquas, and such. I don't hear names like yours too often around here."

"She's in heaven now," I blurted. "My grandmother, that is. Not Shaniqua or the other chick."

Shut up, Emme.

Mother Nicole crossed herself. "Memory Eternal."

I nodded, 'cause I had no idea how I was supposed to respond. "Mother Nicole, what's a *morena*?"

"That's my godson flirting."

I looked at him stretched out supine on the sofa. He acted like he didn't hear her—probably so he didn't have to admit or deny it.

"For real. What does it mean, Mother Nicole?"

"He was saying you're a very pretty, dark-skinned girl."

I felt a tiny stab of pain in my heart.

"Yeah. I got the dark-skin thing all my life. Sometimes people were pretty mean."

"That's awful."

"I got used to it, but if Francis ever says, 'The darker the berry, the sweeter the juice' so help me, I'm gon' smack him."

"You do that. And then I'll smack him. But you don't need to worry. I trained him well. He's very respectful. And it's pretty amazing that you resemble his—"

Francis blurted, "I don't say stuff like that."

Uh-huh. He didn't want her giving me any inside info. But I had my own tricks. "He thinks I look like his ex."

He bolted up, and swung his legs off the cushions. "I never said who you reminded me of."

Mother Nicole chimed in with a grin. "I'm certain he wasn't referring to an ex, lovie."

He shot her a look that I interpreted meant *be quiet*.

I would have tried to press them for information, but I could tell that was all she wrote. Not that his look withered Mother Nicole. On the contrary. She returned his scowl with a smirk.

I liked Mother Nicole. It seemed like she could handle herself. Like Francis, she had soft eyes. Hers were the kind of hazel that changes colors, sometimes looking more gray or green depending on . . . whatever. She was kinda chubby, but in a good way, like you wanna see a nun. Huggable. Short. And she wore cool glasses.

I could already tell she had a great sense of humor. She was, like, joyful.

I checked out her habit. I didn't know much of anything about nuns. "Do you sleep in that stuff?"

She said very seriously, "Yes. We never take our habits off. We have to shower dressed like this so God won't see us naked. And we air-dry in the sun. That's not too bad, except in the winter."

I must have looked crazy because she cracked up. "Of course I don't sleep in this, silly. I'm about to start my day with the Divine Services."

"Oh, do you have church in your office in the morning?"

"No, lovie. The Divine Services is another way of saying the Daily Offices or Liturgy of the Hours."

"What're those?"

She gave me an indulgent smile without a trace of *dang, you're stupid*, in it, even though I felt dumb as rocks.

"It's fixed-hour prayer, lovie. We pray at set times every day. It's a tradition that grew out of the book of Acts, when Peter and John prayed in the temple daily. Before that really. Psalm 119:164 says, 'Seven times a day I praise you for your righteous laws.' Since I was awake after your phone call I prayed the last of the night vigil prayers. And now that it's almost five I'm going to say my morning prayers."

"What? You, like, pray every half-hour or hour or something?"

"I don't do the daily offices that often, but in my line of work, prayer without ceasing is good."

"I know that's what the Bible says. I just wish I knew how to do it. I mean, me and God kick it all the time. Like, constantly. But that's not praying without ceasing."

"Bite your tongue!" she said. "I think it's extraordinary that you 'kick it with God.'"

She acted like she said stuff like "kick it" all day, every day.

Mother Nicole went on. "The way you stay in communion with God and the way I do don't have to be the same. God hears all our prayers, even when we're only kickin' it with Him. In fact, He may even prefer that. Jesus rejected wordy prayers said to impress others."

Francis said, "I like to kick it with the Lord too, but don't get me wrong. I love me some Liturgy of the Hours. Maybe even more." He laced his fingers behind his head and yawned. "Mother Nicole is crazy cool, isn't she?"

"Yeah, she is. I see why you didn't mind her being your girlfriend."

She threw her head back, laughter bubbling up from inside. "Emme, I think you're more Frankie's type than I am." Her gaze shifted to him. "What do you say, Frankie?"

He squirmed on the sofa like Mother Nicole had on X-ray glasses and could see his drawers. "It's not like that." He unlaced his fingers and leaned toward her.

She raised an eyebrow. Didn't say a word. He rushed on with, "I'm thinking about asking her to join us in the *work*."

All Mother Nicole's teasing disappeared. Her mouth flew open. "The *work*? What on earth would make you think such a thing? I understand you miss being around people your own age, but, Frankie, you can't be serious."

He crossed his arms at her rebuke. "But, Mother Nicole—"

"No buts, Frankie. Miguel didn't even want you involved. You know how hard we had to work to get him to let you in. And you know how dangerous it is. And intense. Not to mention . . . *icky*. He's not going to let her work with us."

"Mama Nick, she can see demons. Literally. I've seen her in action."

Okay. Now the brotha was telling my business, and I was gon' have to jump him if he didn't, like, cease and desist, immediately. "Hold up," I said. "First of all, I don't appreciate you telling all that or talking like I'm not even sitting here."

Francis looked at me, his shoulders falling. "I'm sorry, I got so excited—"

Mother Nicole leaned forward. "I apologize too, Emme. He shocked me and I spoke without thinking."

"What kind of work are y'all talkin' about, anyway? Dangerous and intense is bad enough, but *icky*? He didn't say anything to me about any *work*. He told me he wanted me to come over here so I could have a safe place to sleep tonight, and that's it." I looked from one to the other and they averted their eyes like I'd asked them to tell me their darkest secrets. "Is somebody gon' answer me?"

Mother Nicole looked at Francis. "Why don't you tell your friend about the *work*?"

Francis rubbed his hands together. He looked like he was gon' be straight with me. "We do the work of deliverance from satanic bondage. We're part of Father Miguel's team, Emme. He's not simply a priest; he's an exorcist."

"And what? You expect me to be the *Exorsistah* or something? I told you, *I* can't even control it."

Mother Nicole choked back laughter. "Did you say the Exorsistah?"

"Sorry. I was mad."

She hooted as she got up from the reclining chair. "That's funny." For a moment she paused, and then cackled again. "It hits you in waves . . . the *Exorsistah.*" Seeing her so amused broke some of the tension between the three of us.

Some of it.

"It *was* kinda clever," I said.

"And that came to you on the spot?"

I nodded.

"Don't let Father Miguel hear you say that. He'll have a heart attack, and he's already sick enough."

Francis perked up, "Yeah, ma. I could see him now, clutching his heart and moaning about tradition."

"And cursing you in Spanish. Lord, have mercy!" Mother Nicole added. "I need to get ready for the Divine Services. I'd invite you to come, but I think you and Frankie need to get some sleep."

She stepped over to me and patted me on the shoulder. "God give you peace, lovie." For a moment she watched me with a thoughtful expression on her face. "You're more than welcome to stay with us. And you may eat here. I insist. You'll love the food."

"For real?"

"For real. I'm glad Francis brought you." She paused a moment. "Can you really see demons like he said? Literally?"

"I can't help it, Mother Nicole. If I could make it go away I would."

Mother Nicole placed her hand on her heart. She looked at me like that was one of the saddest things she ever heard. "May the Lord have mercy on you, my dear girl." She turned her gaze to Francis still lounging against the armrest. "I need to pray."

Seven

I got up from the wing-backed chair and stood in front of Francis, one hand on my hip. "You tricked me."

"How?"

"You said that y'all could help me."

"We can, but you'd be a powerful asset to us too, Emme."

My voice rose with my irritation. "I ain't havin' nothing to do with casting out demons with y'all! If you think because I can see 'em I want to do that for a livin', you got another think comin', bro'."

"Calm down, Emme."

He got up from the sofa with such graceful, confident ease you'd think there wasn't nothing to getting me chilled out. My stomach did a backflip. Man, he wasn't just fine, he was . . . sexy. And I never thought that about anybody.

Mother Nicole might have had him nervous, but he wasn't stud'in' me. "Thinking of you joining us was just a thought." He didn't seem fazed by my reaction. Totally in control of the situation.

That didn't matter. I wasn't doin' it. He didn't know Emme like he thought he did. I called him on his game. "You had that in mind the whole time, didn't you?"

"How could I not, Emme? It's an extraordinary gift."

"It ain't a gift! If anything, it's a curse. It took my mama away from me. In fact, it got *me* locked up in the crazy house with her when I was twelve. Gifts don't get you put on lockdown. And they don't take your mama away from you."

His eyes filled with golden compassion. He tried to touch my hand but I yanked it away. "Don't be touching me, *Frank*."

"Okay, Emme. I'm sorry. Tell me what happened to your mother."

He was standing so close. And I felt nervous in a whole different way than I did when Ray pushed up on me. This was kinda nice. Delicious even.

I pulled my mind back into focus. "My mama could see demons like I did. And then she started seeing a lotta stuff I couldn't. Stuff didn't *nobody* see but her. She started going what you would call *loco* in your ghetto Spanglish." I start circling my finger by my head. "*Loco!* Do you understand? Crazy! The next thing I knew, I was a ward of the state."

I started feeling claustrophobic. The room seemed to be shrinking. I wasn't breathing right. My breath barely seeped out my lungs.

I'd told him about Mama.

I felt like all my pores had opened wide, and my soul was in danger of escaping. "I gotta get outta this place."

He spoke tenderly. "Emme?"

I didn't want to give him any softness. I was afraid of what would happen. I couldn't move. "What?"

"It was only a thought."

"I don't want nothin' to do with it."

He continued to speak, his voice soothing as a warm fireplace on a wintry night. "Okay, *chica.*"

"They started attacking me when I was five years old, Francis."

"It's all right."

Now my breath came in sharp puffs while my heart slammed against my ribs. I felt like I was standing at the edge of a precipice about to fall into a black abyss. And then I did.

I'm a little thing. In my bed asleep. I feel cold. I stir awake, and I'm about to call my mama, but something feels wrong about the room. It feels like somebody is in there with me, and it isn't Mama.

I look at my VCR clock. It's three thirty in the morning.

I'm too scared to sit up, so I open my mouth to call her; but before one syllable gets out, a black cloud is on top of me. It feels like it's choking and crushing me at the same time. I can't move any part of my body. A scream catches in my mouth. I'm pinned to the bed. That's when the cloud turns into some kind of scaly, reptilian beast. It seems like its head is made of teeth. Teeth as big as knives and just as sharp.

My other senses kick in. I smell it. The worst stench imaginable. I want to throw up, but it's like I'm numb. I can't move any part of my body and even my gag reflex is frozen under the weight of this thing. The giant mouth opens, and it's big enough to devour my whole head.

I feel the tears squeeze out of my eyes. I want to pray, but I can't think of any words. Everything is happening so fast. I hear this soft but urgent voice tell me to move something, any part of my body, but I can't. I can't move at all. I hear the beast on top of me growl. With all my might I try to move my finger. Just one finger.

And I do. Then I unfreeze and scream until my mother comes into the room pleading the blood of Jesus to protect me with its mighty covering.

~

Francis put his hand lightly on my forearm. "Come back, Emme." His voice draws me to the present.

Heck-e-naw.

Francis's hands cupped my elbows, stroking them with the pads of his thumbs, back and forth. His voice like honey now, so sweet and easy going down I could almost taste it. "Why don't I show you where you can rest? Huh?"

"No!"

"Emme," he says, slowly. "You need some sleep."

It took a few moments for my breathing to steady. His gentle touch moved up my arms, but amazingly, I didn't feel invaded like I did with Ray. My inside alarms didn't go off.

He moved in a little closer.

Man, I was feelin' him.

"Chiara," he whispered.

"I don't know what that means."

"It means bright. Shining. Nothing like the darker the cherry the sweeter the juice. Okay?"

I didn't know why I trusted him, but I did.

"I'm tired."

"You're home, now."

"I don't have a home."

"You do now. Come on." He offered me his hands and I took them without resisting. Fatigue threatened to sink me into the ground.

"I can't work with demons." I knew I sounded like a pouty little girl, but I couldn't help it. "Don't try to force me."

"I won't."

"You promise you ain't gon' make me do nothin' I don't want to do?"

And I did mean *nothing.*

"I promise." In his sad eyes I saw he was telling the truth.

With that he led me to his room, which Mother Nicole had prepared for me. I climbed onto his bed and fell into a blessed sleep almost as soon as my head hit the pillow.

My eyes fluttered open.

I didn't know where I was at first. I woke up bleary-eyed in an unfamiliar room, a sweet, musky-scented cologne surrounding me. *Oh yeah . . . now I remember.* Whatever aftershave Francis wore lingered on his pillow. It was like rich earth, with a hint of vetiver, and something spicy and warm. I put it over my face and inhaled.

Why does he live with a priest and a nun?

Maybe his mama or daddy was close to them. But he said his mama didn't want him to be Catholic. She probably wouldn't have wanted him living in a parish house with a priest.

I fluffed the pillow and put my head back on it, rolled to my side and tucked my hands under my cheek.

I could see a crucifix on the wall across from me. Statues of saints and pretty, holy looking pictures covered his walls. He had all kinds of candles and stuff. Like his room was a shrine. It was what I imagined a monk's room would look like.

I eased myself up from his twin-size bed to explore his room. I opened the top drawer of his dresser, being nosy. He was a boxer man. I peeked in the closet. Judging by the color of his gear, he thought he was a monk.

In the corner stood a tall, wooden bookcase, its shelves overflowing. The selection of Bibles alone was impressive: the King James Version. The New Revised Standard Version, The Message. Today's New International Version.

Brotha had a Renovare Study Bible, a Catholic Devotional Bible, an Orthodox Study Bible, a Jerusalem Bible, and a Thompson Chain Reference.

He had all kinds of study helps to go with his Bible collection. He wasn't playin' around!

He also had books about exorcism: *Hostage to the Devil. The Vatican's Exorcist. An Exorcist Tells His Story.* All kinds of freaky-deaky titles.

What had I gotten myself into? He was cute and everything, but not enough for me to want to be dealing with demons all the time.

Someone rapped at the door. Before I had a chance to say anything, it flew open. An older sistah stood there, taking up almost all the room in the doorway. Not necessarily because she was so big—and don't get me wrong, she *was* big—but because so much personality exploded from her and filled up the rest of the space.

Her hot pink T-shirt read "Kiss the Cook." Her hair suffered from a bad dye job and sported about five different shades: red, blond, orange, and brown, with a little black at the roots. She held a plate of food that smelled so good I started salivating.

"Come on, girl, I made you some fried apples and chicken. You done slept the day straight through." She didn't just talk. Her voice blared with the force of a trumpet. Almost made my hair blow back. "They told me you wasn't no bigger than a minute. By the time I finish wit'chu, you gon' be big as me."

I stood there, blinking in shock.

"Come on! You ain't deaf. I ain't gon' sign it for you. *Follow me!*"

I snapped to and scurried behind her like Jesus Himself had called. I had to hustle to keep up with her while she talked the whole time.

"I'm Penny Pop."

I smiled at the irony.

She didn't miss a beat.

"After we eat we gon' do something 'bout that head o' yourn. Honey, that boy done brought you home. You gots to be pretty for him. And he got good hair! You can't be 'round here looking like Whoopi Goldberg. I ain't sayin' her hair ain't right. I'm just sayin' . . . you can't be 'round here lookin' like her. We some Vivica Fox kind of womens, you and me."

She patted her awful hair.

"My real name Georgette, but folk been callin' me Penny since I was little."

She used to be little?

When she walked her butt swung up and down—east and west, east and west—I could hardly keep up with her. For a big girl she sho' could move.

"Why do they call you Penny?"

She stopped her perpetual motion. "I don't know. It don't sound nothin' like Georgette, do it? I don't think much about it now."

The bicoastal swinging started up again, and off we went

through the house, ending up in the kitchen—which smelled heavenly.

Penny Pop busied herself getting me settled at the table. She placed my plate in front of me like a waitress at a diner.

I picked up my fork and was ready to dive in when she put her soft hand on my arm. "We don't eat till we pray 'round here."

I bowed my head.

"Jesus wept," she said. "Now eat. I don't believe it take all day to bless the food. That Frankie? Let him say grace, and we there forty-five minutes. Mother Nicole ain't no better. She got to say the Lord's Prayer and 'bout ninety-nine *Lord, have mercies.* Food be cold by then."

I stifled a laugh and dove into the fried apples, smothered chicken and rice, string beans—and not the kind that comes out of a can—and corn on the cob drenched in butter and salt.

I stole some looks at Penny Pop while she engaged in her busywork around the cozy and homey kitchen. Mismatched styles cozy. I liked it. She looked like she was in her early fifties but hadn't grown all the way up—in a good way. She seemed like the kind of person you'd want to sit next to at a party. Shoot. Penny Pop *was* the party.

"This food is tastin' so good, Penny Pop."

"Girl, I put my foot in that chicken. You might taste a lil' toe jam in the gravy."

I paused a moment, my chicken-loaded fork hovering over the plate, trying not to think about Penny Pop's toe jam. That's when Penny's sound track of continuous gossip began. She plunged herself onto one of the chairs at the table so she faced me, giving me the scoop on everybody, whether or not my inquiring mind wanted to know.

First, the man of the house.

"The old man? Miguel? That's Father Rivera. Now he's sick. He got cancer, God bless him. And it don't look like he got long to live. He don't do much no more. Medicine make him sleep most the time. Which is good, 'cause baaaaby, that's one cranky old man."

"For real?"

"Yeah, girl. He don't know how blessed he is that he got Frankie to help him. Lord only knows why that boy wanna do that kinda work. Look like to me he tryna take it over. But the old man won't have nuthin' to do wit' it. See, Frankie ain't Catholic just yet, an' Father Miguel don't believe nobody but a priest with the authority of the Church—wit' a capital 'C,' baby—can cast the devil out no way. An exorcist in spuh-cific."

"What about what the Bible says about the signs following them that believe? Doesn't that mean all believers can cast out demons?"

"He say only priests can do *exorcism*. That's on a whole 'nother level. Tho' other folk can pray for deliverance. And Miguel don't move from that. Umm-um. And po' Frankie, he wanna be just like that man when he grow up, 'cept he wanna be better than him. Only Father Rivera don't want him to be."

I stabbed at my string beans. "So do he and Francis get along?"

"Francis?"

"I mean Frankie."

"Girl, naw they don't get along. That old cuss can't get along wit' nobody but me and Mother Nicole, and that's only 'cause we don't take nothin'. Frankie too busy tryna please him. He wanna be a priest, you know."

"He wants to be a *priest*?" I almost choked on my corn. I got to coughin', and Penny Pop got to smackin' me on my back like she was Bamm-Bamm on *The Flintstones.*

I couldn't stop her from pounding on me because I was too busy choking to death. I leapt from the chair and grabbed my water to try and drink some, but Penny Pop grabbed my arm and waved it over my head, slinging me around so she could knock my rib cage across the room. My water sloshed a tidal wave over me, until finally I got myself right. "*Priest?* What do you mean he wants to be a priest?"

Penny Pop started stroking my hair and loving on me as if she hadn't been trying to kill me two seconds ago. "You all right, baby? You need some more water?"

"You mean a priest like a don't-ever-get-married *Catholic* priest?"

"Umm-hmm. Fine as that boy is. You know that's gon' break some women's hearts."

"I think it's breaking mine!"

I started feeling warm all of a sudden. I wished I could whip off layers of clothes, but I only had my black baby-doll T-shirt and the Apple Bottoms I had on last night. It would be a bad idea to be standing in the kitchen in my drawers.

"I don't feel good, Penny Pop."

"What's wrong, baby?"

"One of my possible futures just got significantly less interesting. With fewer people in it. It's minus one fine bro' and my babies. Oh, Lord! All my babies are gone!"

She started laughing. "Girl you ain't thinkin' 'bout no babies right now."

"I know! Shoot. But yo, our *potential* was the bomb! I'm all messed up over here now. Emme Vaughn can't have no ghetto *Thorn Birds* babies. That ain't right, Penny Pop." I shook my head trying to get her foul news outta my head. "I was just startin' to think that maybe there might be some brotha worth dreamin' about out here. But Emme Vaughn don't dream about priests."

"Well, don'tchu go givin' up yet," she said, chuckling so hard she wiped tears with a corner of her apron.

"You're laughing, but he was starting to look good to me. My arms are too short to box with God. If I had some normal competition, sistah to sistah, I could probably hold it down, but I can't stand between him and God."

"Girl, you ain't got to stand between him and God. The boy is 'bout meant to be a Catholic priest as I am, and we all know it. He's a young man who got a daddy wound is all. He needs male attention. Maybe he needs you to show him he ain't called. Maybe that's why you here, lil' sis, 'cause he sho' ain't brought nobody else home."

"Naw, that ain't why I'm here."

"Well, we'll see, won't we? Don't you worry yo' pretty head about it."

I got back to eating the great food, and Penny Pop started cleaning up the water I'd spilled in her immaculate kitchen.

"And Mother Nicole," she says as though we had no interruption, "she ain't even no Catholic. She one of them Eastern Orthodox nuns. She and Father Rivera is old friends, and she here for his hospice care."

"Yeah, uh, Frankie told me he's dying, like, soon."

"Girl, I don't wanna claim that. I'm just tellin' you why she here, spuh-cific. She had to get special permission from her head nun or Mother Superior or somethin'. Chile, I forget what they call 'em. I can't hardly see the difference between the Catholics and the Orthodoxes no way, but them two'll stay up all night arguing about *filioque* or *cloissione*—sump'in. I forget what. They love each other to death, though."

She whirled around doing this and that, and a whole lot of nothing. "She been involved with the *work* ever since Frankie recruited her. That boy is crazy 'bout her. He ain't had no mother love since his mama died. And Mama Nick got the discernment of spirits, too. She be done cut right through yo' garbage. That woman is real. That's what make her an excellent nurse, nun, and certified addictions counselor."

"Dang. That's tight."

"Yeah. She the bomb."

"No wonder Francis—I mean, Frankie likes her so much."

"Umm-hmm. Now, tell me about you. Like I said, Frankie don't bring nobody here. He takes they butt right to the Detroit Rescue Mission. And that boy gave up his bed? Umm-umm-umm." She wagged her head as if in wonderment. "Y'all gon' fall in love. I'm telling you, I knows stuff. Now go'ne and tell me 'bout yo'self. I can see you gorgeous. What else 'bout you made him brave enough to bring you home to the ol' man?"

"Ain't nothin' special about me, Penny Pop. I found myself in a bad situation last night, and he was nice enough to help me out."

She turned around and looked me up and down. "Honey, I done told you, he slips folks in a bad situation a bill and takes 'em to the Detroit Rescue Mission or COTS. He don't bring 'em home. Baby, you got something Frankie wants."

"He wants me for the *work*."

"The *work* is almost over, baby. That's gon' go with Father Miguel. I'm thinkin' it ain't the *work*."

Shoot. She made me think that maybe this was about more than me seeing demons. And for the first time in my life, I liked the thought of something like that. "I wish I knew what it was he asked me here for Penny Pop," I said. "And I ain't never lied about that."

Eight

As I finished eating, Penny Pop got started on my head. I usually like natural styles, but she wasn't havin' it. That woman washed, blow-dried, flat-ironed, and curled the ends of my hair faster than I could say "cornrows." Had my junk hanging down my back as silky and straight as it used to look when my mama did it.

Now we were kickin' it at the kitchen table, Penny Pop chattering away, until she suddenly stopped mid-sentence. She started humming some kind of Negro spiritual or something, and I tried to figure out what was up with the behavioral change. It finally occurred to me that she probably had that gossip thing down to, like, a science, and she knew when somebody was about to bust in on the session.

The door opened and Francis held it so this frail-looking old Latino man could enter. He was fair-skinned and wore all black with a white clerical collar. I could tell Francis was a little bit nervous about introducing me, and I thought, *Dang, I only slept here for a few hours. It wasn't even my idea to come. Don't you worry none, Francis. I'll be on my way as soon as I can get up outta here.*

But the old dude, he, like, froze when he looked at me. Gasped. I wondered if he was sucking his last breath.

Francis ignored it and said, "Father Miguel Rivera, this is Miss Emme Vaughn."

Before I could formulate the right thing to say he went off!

He yelled like I was a ghost, and not the Holy one. "*¿Qué maldad es ésta? Has traído a hogar tu madre.*" Then he practically collapsed into Francis's arms.

"No, Padre," Francis said, but the man still looked faint, like something about me made him feel worse than he did before he walked into the room.

I looked at Penny Pop. Her eyes told me everything would be okay, but I felt like pond scum.

The old man started sobbing, "*¡Dios mio! ¡Ella es la imagen de tu madre!*" His body quaked and heaved with emotion.

Tears came to *my* eyes. An' I didn't even know what I was supposed to be cryin' about.

Francis tried to hustle the man out of the kitchen. But Father Rivera pulled himself together, as though embarrassed by his outbursts. He straightened up, spun around, and stormed out—in a feeble way—shouting at Francis, "*¡Ella no puede permanecer aquí! ¡Ella debe ir!*"

It sounded like Francis argued with him. "*Por favor darte una ocasión, Papi. Ella no tiene dondequiera ir.*"

He shot me a quick look before they went down the hall. I didn't know what to say. I looked at Penny Pop. "What was that all about?"

"I don't know, girl. He went straight up Ricky Ricardo on

you. I know one thing, I ain't seen him upset like that in a long time."

"Could you make out any of the words?"

"I know *madre* mean mama. *Papi* and *padre* mean Daddy. That's about it. I don't speak no Spanish. The old man mostly speaks in English. He only go off like that when he mad. You got some extra bad trouble wit' yo' mama and daddy, lil' sis?"

"That's an understatement. But why would that make *him* so upset?"

"I don't know what that there was about. But I'm sho' gon' find out."

"You find out all you want, Penny Pop," I said. "I'm 'bout to bounce."

I still had forty bones. That was forty more than I started with. Somehow I'd figure out the rest.

Nine

I could hear Mother Nicole and Francis in the living room tryna calm the old bro' down. I was pretty upset myself. I told Penny Pop to tell them I said thanks for everything, but I'm *out.*

The best thing about traveling light is that I didn't have to pack when I left.

I wanted to say good-bye to Francis, and even Mother Nicole. I'd never met a nun, and she was kinda fun. But I couldn't forge no attachments. I needed to fortify myself to survive in the streets again. Out there you can't get too close to nobody, and you couldn't trust folks as far as you could throw 'em.

Penny Pop asked me to wait, but I told her I didn't have that kind of time. It was almost evening now. And I was in Inkster, where too many people knew me and knew that my mama was locked up. I had to get my bearings and figure out where I'd spend the night.

Penny Pop said she wanted to give me something, but instead of waiting for her to return, I slipped out the back door so I wouldn't have to pass Francis, Mother Nicole, or Ricky Ricardo. I was halfway down the street when I heard my name.

Francis.

I kept walking.

"Wait up," he shouted, tearing down the street after me.

I didn't.

He came trotting beside me like a colt before I knew it. He wasn't even panting.

What was the point in trying to outrun someone who would obviously catch me anyway? I stopped.

"What?"

He looked at me like I was crazy. "You're just gonna leave without saying good-bye?"

"I told Penny Pop to tell you 'bye."

He gave me the golden eyes, looking all fine and bright. "You're leaving me? After all we've been through?"

Despite the fact that I felt defensive, he was so charming he actually got a smile out of me. But I couldn't act like the old man hadn't gone off on a sistah. "Obviously the good reverend has a problem with me. I ain't tryna be no place else I ain't wanted. I, like, been dealing with that since I was twelve."

He took my hand. "It's not that, Emme."

"I don't have to speak Spanish to know I'm a problem."

"I talked to him. It's okay now."

"Not for me."

I started walking again. Not that it kept him from joining me.

"You surprised him, that's all."

"Why, because you brought a girl home, Mr. Priest Wannabe?"

He didn't turn his gaze away from me. "I knew Miss Penny would tell you that."

"Why didn't you tell me?"

"It's complicated, Emme."

"It's not a secret, is it? I mean, you told me about your mama and daddy being Catholic and that you were being initiated or whatever. You told me yo' daddy broke yo' mama's heart. You could have told me you want to be a priest. What if I was diggin' you? You ever think about that?"

"I told you I'm too old for you."

"You liked it, Francis. Didn't you? You ain't gotta answer, because I know you enjoyed flirting."

He didn't answer. Now he did look away. "Come back inside where we can talk. Please."

"You're playin' games."

"I'm not. Let's go inside where we can talk in private."

I snatched my hand out of his. "I'm gettin' away from here. From you and Father Ricky Ricardo and your *whack* demon obsession. I don't need this. A'ight?"

"You do need a place to stay where you'll be safe."

"It looks like this ain't that place."

I picked up speed to get away from him. And that was supposed to be that, because my soul was tired. I didn't have time for anybody's crazy agendas. It hadn't been twenty-four hours, but already it seem like somebody was tryna use me. I didn't have anything left. I took a few weary steps away from him. Then he said it.

"Emme! What if I said *I* need you? *I* want you to stay. Not just for the *work*."

I stopped. "Why do you need me, Francis? Why should I stay?"

He paused. Looked at the ground, thinking. Struggling. When he finally spoke, it didn't clarify anything. "I just do. I don't know what else to say." He looked at me, his eyes searching. "You're ev—" He shook his head, not finishing his sentence.

"You talk a blue streak any other time, brotha. W'sup with you now?"

"I need you, *and* we're good together. Isn't that enough?"

"Define 'together,' Francis."

"We were good together in that store. Don't you wanna see what the possibilities are? What God can do through us serving Him as a team? Everybody who loves God wants to do His will. You can't tell me the thought doesn't appeal to you."

He had a point. But . . . "I ain't tryna do anything with demons."

"Then don't. That's not the only way to serve God. I said I wouldn't force you."

"What was that old man shouting about?"

"He's trippin'. He always thinks I have some kind of ulterior motive. Stay a few days. Rest up. Think this through. That's all I'm asking for. You can't beat that. Can you?"

"What do you want from me, brotha, if you know I ain't about to get on your team?"

"I'm trying to do the works of Jesus. Remember, I'm supposed to be taking care of his little one. Let me help you."

"I'm supposed to believe you just want to do God's work? Something not demon-related. I saw all those crazy demon books in your room. *You're* the dang-gone demon hunter. That's why you asked me about that book in Walgreen's."

"I have those books because I work with an exorcist and I want to understand what we do. And if you wanna know the truth, I don't do much. I'm the muscle. I hold people down when they're going crazy with demon strength. I don't even get to do as much as we did in the store. So it ain't all that. Can you come back inside? Father Miguel calmed down. Emme, I wouldn't let anybody hurt you, including him. I only thought you could help because the case we're about to work on involves a teenager. Same age as you. She needs help, but if you're not the person to do that, it's okay."

Again, I searched his eyes. It didn't look like he was tryna play me. "Okay," I said.

A wide smile spread across his face, the dimple appearing. "Cool. Shall we?" He motioned with his head toward the house.

I went back with him. Despite how leery I was, I didn't have a better option.

Ten

When we got back inside, I could almost see the tension like I could demons. He happily chatted while we trekked down the hall—like I'm all ready to sign up for whatever.

He noticed my lack of enthusiasm.

"Can we just *talk* about the *work*? No pressure. I never had a friend interested in this stuff that wasn't an old white person."

"You still don't have one."

He ignored my dis.

"I'm hoping the bishop will expedite the process of approving the exorcism of this girl, or Father Miguel is gonna be too sick to perform the rite. Plus she's in bad shape. Her parents are *through.* They've done all they could with the little they have. Can't get much help for anything when you're broke and living in the hood."

He spoke so fast it sounded almost like he said it all in one breath. "Father Rivera and I don't agree on a lot of things. Actually, we don't agree on most things. I believe in the priesthood of *all* believers. He stands by tradition with a big 'T.' And I see his point. But you know, God works through and then beyond tradition. I'm trying to figure out what God is doing next. What will the next-generation exorcist look like?"

He squeezed my hand. "Maybe they'll be an *exorsistah* in the future."

"As long as it ain't me."

"Stay open, Chirara. I had to have met you for a reason."

"It ain't *that* reason."

He pulled me into the living room, halting our discussion.

I tried to subtly pull my hand out of his, but he wouldn't let go. I didn't like that feeling. He knew I was a runaway. He said he could *see* what had happened with the men in my past. I thought he'd understand that I don't like feeling like somebody is forcing me to do something. Especially when it comes to touching. I was tired of being manipulated by men, and I didn't want somebody holding my hand when I didn't want it to be held. But I didn't want to cut a fool in front of his people. I had to talk to my inner self—"He's holding your hand. That's all"—to keep from goin' off on him.

He leaned over and whispered in my ear, "Chill, Emme. I know what your concerns are. I'm showing you that I've got you. It's a unity move. That's all."

I relaxed my hand and stopped resisting him.

I looked up to see Father Rivera and Mother Nicole watching us. I couldn't have been more self-conscious if I'd stepped onto the stage during amateur night at the Apollo.

Mother Nicole sat by the old man on the sofa. I thanked God for that woman. Those hazel eyes shone with compassion for me, in contrast to Father Rivera's suspicious gaze. His eyes were light too, almost like Francis's, but more the color of amber. The kind you see bugs trapped for thousands of years in. I imagined myself stuck in those hard eyes.

I nodded a greeting to them. The old man nodded in return. Mother Nicole said in stark contrast to our brusque mannerisms, "Hello, Emme. How did you sleep, lovie?"

"I slept fine, Mother Nicole. Did your prayers go okay?"

Her face lit up like she didn't expect me to ask about that. "They sure did. I prayed for you, too. God assured me He had you in the palm of His hand."

"Thanks."

I turned my focus to the ground because something about the tenderness in her voice and eyes touched my heart when she said that. Man, I felt so weary. But I didn't want them to see me go all soft, especially the old man.

"Make yourself comfortable, Emme," Francis said, and he gestured to the sofa next to Mother Nicole. He stood in the middle of the room and put his spin on my being there.

"Father Miguel, once again, this is Emme Vaughn. She's cool people, but things are a little rough for her. I've told you both a little about her, how I met her at Walgreens last night. I told you about the housing trouble she has right now and also about the extraordinary gift she has to see into the spirit world." He turned to me. "Emme, maybe you can tell them more about it."

I cut my eyes at him.

The old man spoke. "Do you have to coach her through this? Can't she speak for herself?"

Mother Nicole warned, "Father Miguel . . ."

But he tore right into me, and not about being homeless. "What is this so-called gift, young lady?"

I yanked on my emotional armor. "I never said I had a gift. Holla at yo' boy about that."

"My boy?"

Mother Nicole answered, "She means your *friend,* Miguel."

Father Miguel gave me another verbal nudge. Or push. "Come, come now. Don't be modest. I don't think Frank would have brought you here if he didn't have some ridiculous notion about you being involved in our *work*. Or is there some other reason he had you in his bed, Miss Vaughn?"

Mother Nicole said more firmly this time, *"Miguel!"*

I decided to let that go for Mother Nicole's sake. Francis could tell that man was tickin' me off though. He tried to reassure me with his eyes. "Just tell him how it works, Emme, so he can drop the subject and we can get on to the social justice stuff we're supposed to be about because we're followers of Christ." He gave Father Rivera a hard look and me a kind one. "Okay, Emme?"

I addressed Father Rivera. "I already told him I don't know how it works. It's like the veil between heaven and earth gets lifted, and I can see into spirit worlds. Why or how, I couldn't tell you. Why don't you ask God? Ain't y'all 'sposed to be tight like that?"

"You watch your tone with me, Miss Vaughn. This is *my* house."

"With all due respect, Father Rivera, I left your house a few minutes ago. I'm only here because Francis begged me to come back. And he said we weren't gon' deal with this."

Father Miguel paled. "He told you his name is Francis?"

I decided not to give him all our secrets, and hoped Francis hadn't. "How else would I know it?"

He gave Francis a withering stare, which bro' ignored like he did a good many of my questions.

"What else did he tell you?"

"That I could get some help here. Apparently, he was wrong."

Mother Nicole intervened. "This isn't a war between you and Emme, Miguel. She's just a teenager, and she needs help. She doesn't deserve your completely unacceptable contempt. And Emme, Father Miguel isn't a foster parent intent on exploiting you. He has concerns because he doesn't know you. That's understandable. You may want to soften that edge of yours."

God, forgive me.

I felt bad. My mama raised me to respect my elders, but this man tripped on me from the first moment he looked at me, and my nerves were frayed. "I'm sorry," I muttered, but I meant it.

If Father Rivera felt bad, he didn't offer a word of apology to let anybody in the room know it.

Whatever.

Mother Nicole gave me her attention. "So, Emme, it seems God wills this to happen as He sees fit?"

I shrugged again. I'm sure I looked as sullen and surly as I felt. I didn't want to talk about this. "I guess."

She rocked back against the cushions and adjusted herself. "I wonder if the spiritual disciplines would help her tune in to it more? Sharpen her spiritual antennae, so to speak."

This idea seemed to excite Francis. "That's what I wondered, too!" He caught himself and tamed that enthusiasm. "But she doesn't want to get involved with that ministry. I can't blame her, but I couldn't help but think if she did want to work with us, part of her training should be the classic disciplines. I thought we'd give her the total package: physical, spiritual, and emotional. It would be a whole new thing. Something we've never done."

"Too bad I ain't gon' do it," I said.

Concern shadowed Mother Nicole's face. "I believe her instincts are spot on, Frankie. I know you think Emme is special, but that doesn't mean she's suitable for the *work*, even if she wanted to do it."

"And I don't," I said.

He kinda blushed. "She *is* special to me, Mama Nic, and not just because she can see the spirit world. As far as the *work* is concerned, her gift . . ." He paused, looking buzzed on this idea of me working with them. "I'm sure we could find a way to integrate it."

Father Rivera broke in, shattering Francis's excitement like somebody pouring ice water on him. "It sounds ridiculous! First of all, you don't know if she really has this gift she says she has."

I sighed like the three of them had a habit of doing. "I ain't say I had no gift. Okay?"

Francis told Father Rivera, "I've seen her operating this gift."

I didn't appreciate them talking about me like I was in the kitchen somewhere with Penny Pop.

Father Rivera turned to me. "You don't know what you saw," he challenged.

I tried to keep my respect in order, when what I really wanted to do was slam him. I held my tongue. Francis didn't.

"But, for real, I saw—"

The old man ranted on at Francis. "And now you parade her around here like it's even possible that she could be an exorcist. What does the Church believe, Frank?"

"That only priests can be exorcists."

"And who can perform exorcisms?"

"Priests, and only with the express permission of a bishop."

"And who does that leave out?"

"That leaves out anyone who isn't a priest with a bishop's blessing, including the teams of believers I've been talking about. And women. And *me*, sir."

For a sick person, Father Rivera didn't have any problem administering a smackdown.

"Then get these romantic notions out of your head. Exorcism is an ugly business. You know that, Frank. I never wanted anything to do with it, myself. It's bad enough that you want to be a priest. Why can't you just enjoy being a young man? Even as insolent as she is, I'd rather you be taking her out to dinner instead of trying to get her involved with casting out demons. Let old men do what old men do. And priests do what priests do."

Mother Nicole jumped in the conversation. "He's right, Frankie. It's not that we don't appreciate you. Father Miguel has needed you in these last few cases more than ever. But she's young, very thin, and unseasoned."

The old man looked me up and down like I was nothing. Less than nothing. He spoke to Francis. "She can't do us any good. That you even considered her should be an affront, even to her."

"She's gifted," he said, tryna stay cool. "I know she's thin. That ain't a sin! She's malnourished from fasting like one of the desert Ammas and not having a place she felt safe enough to eat."

"Then take a few days, feed her, and get her out of here."

Francis thrust his hands in his pockets, shook his head, and smiled, like this was some kind of power game they played at.

He rocked on the heel of his Timbs. "I can take her somewhere, but I'll go with her 'cause she's on my watch now. And *I* don't leave vulnerable sistahs hangin'."

The priest didn't say anything. Dude just scowled at Francis. And me.

Francis turned to me. "I'm thinkin' you can stay as long as you need to, Emme," he said. "The good father didn't say anything against us, so I'ma take that to mean he's for us."

With that he grabbed my hand again, and we made a grand exit.

Eleven

I followed Francis through the narrow hallway of the bungalow and into a small bedroom he must've been using for storage. Musical instruments propped on or against boxes stacked halfway up the wall: guitars—acoustic and electric—and a couple of basses. Some funky-looking electronic drum. Mama, Papa, and Baby Bear–size amplifiers. Bro' was serious about his music.

"Dang, boy," I said. "You got everything up in this piece."

"Naw. Not everything, but I'm workin' on it."

"How come you don't keep your instruments in your bedroom? From the looks of your room, I wouldn't have even thought you were a musician."

"I sleep in my room. Read. If I took an instrument in there, I'd end up staying up all night."

A bow-back country stool sat in the center of the room. He pulled it to the side and motioned for me to have a seat.

I sat and watched him get busy, moving from acoustic guitar, to electric, back to acoustic, and finally settle on a bass.

He plugged it into an amplifier, strapped it on, and started tuning it.

"Are you about to serenade me, Francis?"

"Naw," he said grinning and tuning, "I might turn you out, *chica*, and then I won't be able to get rid of you."

"Yeah. I see how hard you been tryna get me out your life. You don't wanna go Usher on me."

"I'ma play bass for you."

"I kinda figured that when you strapped the bass on."

"Quiet, sassy girl."

He didn't just play that bass, though. He, like, became one with it. He made that bass an extension of himself, so that the music wasn't coming out of the instrument. He was the instrument. And he didn't stop there.

Aw, man. His music was, like, transcendent. I watched in openmouthed awe as he plunked, plucked, and picked at the strings in a way that must've made the angels jealous. Francis caressed rhythms out of that baby that went right into the secret place in me where only God lived and once had visited. But I couldn't even trip. The sounds of his music took me to heavenly places, and dang, that was just one bass.

When he stopped, the quiet almost offended me.

For a moment I couldn't speak. He searched my face, for what I wasn't sure. I think he was waiting for me to tell him what I thought, but I couldn't find the words.

Finally he said, "Well?"

"I kinda see what you mean about the turning me out thing."

He looked surprised for a moment. Then we both cracked up.

He got back to the bass, but not what he was doing before. He played the scales, repeating the same boring notes over and over.

"How long do you go through those scales?"

"I spend hours at it sometimes," he said. "It's like prayer. You do it long enough, it's just natural when you have to do something deep. Like spiritual warfare."

"Don't start." I shook my head. "Man. That would drive me crazy."

"It drives Father Miguel crazy, too. I started doing it without the amp so he wouldn't have to hear it, but right now, I'm not feelin' the sensitivity to him. At least for a few minutes."

"You play when you get upset, don't you? It's like that thing you do when somebody is tryna talk to you when you ain't feelin' it. You escape."

"Yeah," he said. "Sometimes I escape into the music in my head. So, it can be double trouble."

"Are you feeling better now?"

"Much better," he said. "Got my God, got my bass, got my exorsistah. A brotha don't need no more than that right now."

I chuckled. "Well, two outta three ain't bad."

Francis said, "What you talkin' about, girl? *God* is with me."

"Father Rivera ain't feelin' no exorsistah."

His fingers continued running scales. "I told you, he thinks I have motivations that I don't have."

"You brought some sistah he don't know nothing about into his home. He probably thinks we're up to no good."

"It's not that. He knows me. If I was gon' do something like that, I'd leave. I wouldn't disrespect his house. This is complicated, Emmy. Don't sweat it."

I could tell he didn't want to talk about it, so I let him play without pressing the issue. He must've wanted to keep me talking though.

"You play any instruments?" he asked.

"I wish. I do a little spoken word to beats. It ain't nothin' like what you doin'. You don't get a chance to do work on that level when you get tossed around a lot. I'm surprised you got to be so good."

"Yeah, well, I got tossed around with my guitar. I put a lot of time into this. And . . ." He looked embarrassed, and maybe a little bashful. "They say I'm a prodigy."

"Are you?"

"I don't know. I understand music. Always did. The language of it. I *speak* music, if you can get that. I've always been that way. It's like how you see in the spirit world. You just do."

"Francis. Don't go there."

I got up from the chair and explored the room while he played. Touched the boxes with names from companies that sell stuff like speakers. Beat boxes. I wondered what he had in those boxes.

My mind kept going back to why I was in that house. I felt a little sad. I knew this wasn't gonna work out. Not for long, no matter how Francis flexed on the old priest.

"He ain't Mr. Nice Guy is he, that Father Rivera?"

He shook his head, and stretched his long legs out in front of him. "He's definitely not easy, but he has his moments."

I sighed, picking up an acoustic guitar. Francis watched me, but not all paranoid like he didn't want me messing around with his stuff. He looked curious.

I strummed a few strings. "Who does he think he is, anyway?

Some kind of super priest? He got powers I don't know about?"

"Nope," he said, still playing the scales.

Scales were kinda gettin' on my nerves, too.

He continued, "Those house slippers hide his feet of clay. But I can't knock his experience. He's a heckuva exorcist, and his results are some of the best in the game. I wouldn't be working with him if he was whack. Or pushing for you to do the same."

The more we talked about it, the more I knew my days of hangin' with Francis were numbered.

"He doesn't like me, and I ain't crazy about him. It was a nice try, but he ain't with your plan. It's cool, though."

"No, it's not, Emme."

"I'll stay a couple of days, but I gotta dip after that, Francis."

He stopped his relentless fingering of bass strings. Stood where he was, his golden eyes looking deeply into mine. My breath hitched.

"I want to share so much with you. Teach you the best things I know." He leaned the instrument against a box. "I want to feed you all kinds of healthy food, teach you everything I know about prayer and the spiritual disciplines. I want to train you in martial arts. Even help you get your GED, if you want. I want to make sure you're the baddest thing the kingdom of God has ever seen. Shield you against the nightmares that you've had to live through since you were a little girl. But I can't do that if you leave."

Shoot. That sounded kinda tight. Then something odd dawned on me. "Why would somebody on an exorcist's team need to know martial arts?"

"Like I said, I'm the muscle. It takes a lot of strength and fortitude to work in deliverance ministry. And on the real, I think you'd be hot as a martial artist."

I saw it. In my mind I was not just kickin' *devil* butt. I was kickin' *a whole lotta* butt. Starting with Ray.

Pow! Pow! Bam!

I put me a list together right quick: all the punks I was in foster care homes with that were just like Ray; Father Rivera—though I went easy on him 'cause Francis liked him, and he was sick; the girl who cut a big chunk of my hair out in the crazy house when I was twelve because she was bald-headed and jealous. I could even kick Francis's butt when he got on my nerves. Or even when he didn't. We could be like Daredevil and Electra in the movie, when they were fighting on that playground when they first met.

I got into my butt-kickin' fantasy so deep I heard Francis's voice, but not what he said to me. "I'm sorry. What?"

He had an amused smirk on his pretty face and now stared at me with one eyebrow raised. "Emme?"

"What, Francis?"

"Not only did I tell you my whole vision of the neo exorcist, I told you my big sob story of getting my GED despite the odds against me, and blah, blah, blah, none of which you heard. You missed me play the violin, while rain fell against the window and a single tear rolled dramatically down my cheek."

I folded my arms across my chest. "I already know exorcisms are physical, and you did *not* cry. It ain't raining, either. I can't enroll in a GED completion program, Francis. They'd find me."

"Emme, I said—which you obviously missed—that I did it on my own, and I'll bet you could, too. Mother Nicole and I could prep you if you stayed. You don't even have to take the test until after your birthday. You don't have to be so scared. It's not like the police are staking out the hood or throwing up roadblocks to find you. You ran away from a foster care home. You're not on the FBI's Most Wanted list."

"I don't care. They found me before, and it can happen again if I ain't careful. This is Inkster. I grew up here. People know me. I ain't tryna go back into foster care thirty-two days before I'm grown. I'll hang with you a few days, but I'm not with the neo exorcist thing."

"All right, Emme. I said I wouldn't force you to do anything. Where you tryna go when you get legal?"

"That ain't your concern."

He stepped up to me, all manly and fine, making my heart rate rival what I bet that electronic drum of his could do. Got right in my face.

"It's my concern now. You won't be out there on your own if I can help it. I'm offering you room and board and an intensive spiritual journey that will give you skills you can use for the rest of your life, but if you won't accept my offer I'll still see you to safety somewhere else. I had hoped that since you're Jamilla's age, you could help her. I'm not sure how, but I got a feeling she's not telling us everything. Sometimes girls tell other girls what they won't tell anybody else. But she's in God's hands."

My heart dropped so fast to my feet I thought it'd stay there permanently.

Jamilla?

He noticed my expression change. "What is it, Emme? Are you okay?"

Naw. It wasn't Jamilla. Not my girl.

"Jamilla is her name?"

"Yeah."

I searched my mind for anything he might have said about this girl. He mentioned we were the same age. Did he say she lived in Inkster? *Dang.* He hadn't said much about her at all. *Aw man! Why didn't I ask him more questions?*

My mouth went dry, and I swallowed what felt like a rock in my throat. I asked him one of the hardest questions I ever asked anybody, even though it was a simple one. I silently prayed he wouldn't say what had to be impossible.

"What's Jamilla's last name?"

"Jacobs. Oh, snap! What was I thinking? You lived in Inkster. Maybe you know her."

Oh, *snap,* my butt. He had to have thought about it. The town was too little, and I said I grew up here.

I put the guitar down and walked away from Francis and back to the chair. He didn't follow me, but gave me a little space instead of hovering over me.

After some time I finally managed to say, "Jamilla Jacobs was my best friend. Since we were in the first grade."

"Emme, I'm so sorry."

Shoot. I was sorry, too. Because now I was staying for sure. If she was possessed, I was gonna kick that devil's butt. I didn't care what I had to do.

Twelve

I sat there in that bow-backed chair, surrounded by boxes and instruments, looking crazy until Francis touched my hand.

"Don't touch me!" I said "Just leave me alone."

Francis backed off. "Sorry, Emme."

"Are you sure it's that? She's *possessed*?"

"I'm sorry, but it's sorta obvious. There's no medical explanation for her symptoms, and our whole team agrees. We don't take cases to the bishop unless we're sure."

He crouched down beside me but didn't touch me. I could tell he felt as helpless as I did. He kept tryna talk to me. "It's only a matter of time—a short time—and we'll have the clearance and can do the exorcism. We're very successful, Emme. I told you, Father Miguel is a great exorcist. One of the best."

I couldn't hide the anguish in my voice. "You said it can take *months* to cast out demons. And I can't even imagine what she's going through."

"It doesn't always take months. And we don't think it'll take that long. Father Miguel doesn't have months."

"What if it doesn't work? I mean, look at that guy at Walgreens."

"He ran out, Emme. Maybe he wasn't willing. People are free to keep their demons if they want to, as bad as that sounds. Jamilla *wants* our help. Or she says she does."

"What's that supposed to mean?"

"She's holding back something. I can feel it. Mother Nicole agrees. That's one reason I thought you could help. Sistah to sistah. But I had no idea y'all were tight like *that.* That's a blessing."

"*If* I were actually on your team!"

"You can be."

"With Father Cranky? Ain't no way! Now, what the heck am I supposed to do?" I got up and began to pace.

"I don't know. We can just work on it."

"Even if Father Foul let me on the team, don't forget I couldn't even get a demon to jet from that man in Walgreens. And I had your help!"

"I told you sometimes it takes time. Some only go out through prayer and fasting, and sometimes that means a lot of prayer and a lot of fasting."

My anxiety shot high as the ceiling. Man! I needed to see my girl. *Badly.* And to tell the truth, I wanted to see her without Francis. I didn't want him tryna scope out if I could see the demon inside of her or do something. I didn't have any skills, really. If I did, I'd have helped my mama. I only dealt with demons when I had to. And that was mostly to keep them away from me. I never really cast a demon out of a person. Not like no sho' 'nuff exorcism. That thing in Walgreens showed me I wasn't as big and bad as I thought I was.

Naw. Jamilla wasn't possessed. This was all crazy. I was on the couch in Kiki's basement asleep, and none of this madness was happening.

Only I wasn't sleep. And I sho' wasn't at Kiki's house.

Even if she wasn't possessed, she must've been doing something to make him and his whole team think she was. Her parents must believe it too, if they were worried enough to get an exorcist involved with her.

What in the heck happened to Jamilla? She knew better than to get into Wicca or use Ouija boards and stuff. She wouldn't be hangin' with no psychics. She was a *good* girl. Did all the right stuff. She knew what I could see and didn't want nothin' to do with that. She knew about my mama. So w'sup with that?

Then I thought about my mama. She was a good person, too. She loved God the best way she could, like most of us. And look at her. Man! I ain't wanna deal with this junk.

That dang-gone Francis! All I wanted was something to eat and a safe place to lay my head down. Maybe find some way to help him out as a DJ or something, and get me some kick-butt diva boots. How was I supposed to walk away now?

Francis annoyed me with his questions. "Are you all right?"

Was he serious?

"*Heck-e-naw*, I ain't all right. You just told me my girl is possessed."

"Do you want me to take you to see her?"

"No. I don't. I don't want you to do nothin'." I tried to soften my tone. "Not right now. I need to be alone, Francis. I need to think."

"Do you want to go somewhere? We can chill at the park or something."

"I said I wanna be alone!"

I needed to chill. That sharp edge Mother Nicole got on my case for was about to slice Francis into julienne potatoes. But I was upset. I didn't want to be with him or anybody.

"I don't know if you should go anywhere alone."

"I'm just gonna take a walk."

He didn't look like he was cool with that. "Let me go with you."

"Stop pressin' me, bro'. I don't want you to go."

Those gold eyes flashed with hurt. But he didn't complain. He didn't close up in himself and start rambling off whatever was in his brain like he did when he didn't want to deal with stuff. Despite me trippin', he was with me.

I tried to calm myself. Take some deep breaths.

As much as I didn't want to be touched, I stopped my pacing and put my hand on his shoulder. He didn't move. "I'm sorry. I didn't mean to yell at you, Francis." I took a few more deep breaths. "I know you're tryna help me. I'm thankful for that. For real."

I meant that. I really was grateful, and I realized a lot of my behavior was what my old psychiatrist would call "acting out." To be honest, I was scared. Too much was happening too soon. "I'm just trippin'. Yo, my life seems to be imploding, and bro', it wasn't a great life to start with."

"How can I help you?"

"I wanna take a walk. Move my body. Clear my head."

"It's gonna be dark soon. You promise you won't stay out too late?"

"Promise."

"And you'll stay away from the hood."

"The hood is across the parking lot, Francis."

"Those aren't the projects I'm talking about. I think you know that. I'll take you to see her, Emme. You need to be prepared for what you'll see if you go over there."

"I just wanna walk. Okay?"

He didn't press me, though I could tell he wanted to. "Don't stray too far."

"How can I? Inkster is only six miles square."

He didn't smile at my attempt at humor.

"Trust me, Francis. Like you asked me to trust you."

"Okay. I'll walk you to the door."

True to his word, that brotha led me out of his practice room and through the house. I don't know where Mother Nicole and Father Rivera were. I didn't care, either. Only one person filled my thoughts.

Francis opened the door for me, and I trotted off the porch and headed the opposite direction away from the parking lot. I walked around the block, back onto Annapolis, and headed across Middlebelt Road to The Gardens—yet another infamous housing project in the little city, and the home of my girl, Jamilla.

I prayed hard as I walked. For both Jamilla and myself. With every paranoid step I took, I wondered if somebody would see me who knew me. I wondered if Antoine was still around, and what I'd do if I saw him. Then again, I hadn't been to Inkster in a long time. Probably wasn't nobody stud'in' me anyway, including Antoine. If he was as smart as I thought he was, he would have busted up out of Inktown a long time ago. And now that I thought about it, even if somebody did say something to me, I didn't have to tell them all my business. Nobody had to know I ran away.

I walked through The Gardens, shocked. My mama said the housing project had once been a model for low-income housing around the nation. Now it was a boarded-up ghost town. Didn't look like hardly anybody lived here now, and I hoped that Jamilla and her folks finally caught a break and moved out.

I crossed Pine Street and found the three-bedroom unit they had lived in. It looked like they were still there. Jamilla's mama loved her little piece of yard. I could tell it was their place by the black-eyed Susans, hostas, and impatiens out front.

I knocked on the door, and Jamilla's mama, Mama Jacobs, looked startled when she saw me. She paused and placed her hand over her heart, before a huge smile spread across her face.

I took in the sight of this woman I loved. Her deep ebony skin just like mine. She always made me feel beautiful. Her Claire Huxtable television mama sassiness, with a little more down southern charm, and a touch of ghetto fabulousness.

"Lord, have mercy. Is that my other chile? Is that you, Emme?"

I wanted to cry, but instead I smiled. "It's me, Mama Jacobs."

She pushed open the screen. And pulled me into a Mama Bear–hug. She rocked me in her soft mama arms, almost suffocating me in her bosoms. "Umph, umph, umph," she said. "Lord, I thought we'd never see you again. You an answer to my prayers."

I just held on. Wasn't nobody like Mama Jacobs and the feeling she always inspired in me, that no matter how far away from home you found yourself, somebody back there loved you. I'd forgotten that. That there were people in this world who loved me.

When we finally let each other go, Mama Jacobs wiped away tears. She looked at me with great tenderness. "How yo' mama doing, baby?"

"She ain't doing too good. About the same." I hadn't heard a word about my mama for two years. But somehow I knew it was true. Mama Jacobs didn't press me for details, thank goodness.

Silence spread between us. I sighed and plunged into it. "Ma, where is Jamilla?"

She wagged her head. "Your girl is in trouble, Em."

Man. She called me Em, like Mama use to.

"I heard."

I saw the shock on her face and wanted to reassure her. "I know Fran—um, Frankie. The guy on the team that's gonna help her. He wanted me to help out, too. He knows about . . . what I can do."

Her face brightened like tinsel on a Christmas tree. "I knew the Lord sent you. I knew you'd be able to help her with your gift."

I didn't even get into it.

"I only know what Frankie told me, Mama Jacobs, and it ain't much. Tell me what you think happened."

"Come in here. Let's have a seat, honey."

I followed her into their home—and it really was a *home*, full of warmth and love and comfort, right there in the heart of the ghetto. They'd gotten some rent-to-own furniture. I could tell it was rent-to-own, because all that rental furniture looked about the same. I sat on the cheap, hideous brown floral couch and sank into the once-familiar feeling of my extended family. The living room set was different, but the place still smelled like Mama Jacobs's cooking. She still wore Love's Baby Soft perfume, which she said she'd worn when she was a teenager. Jamilla wore it, too. She still had dollar-store knickknacks all over the place. And plants. And that picture that used to be in her own mama's living room—a black woman with a big ol' Afro, lying with a tiger. Some things never changed.

But she had. She looked way older than the last time I saw her—older than she should. And way too thin.

She sat across from me in the love seat, checkin' me out the way mamas do. "You done lost weight, Em. Ain't they taking care of you in that foster home?"

"I'm all right, Ma."

"It'a kill yo' mama if she saw how skinny you was."

I didn't need to be talkin' about my mama.

"Please, Mama Jacobs. Tell me about Jamilla."

She shook her head. "Baby, I don't know. She was always a good girl. You know that. She started going away a lot. Said there was this bookstore she liked. And she was always bringing home books, so we thought, she's just reading a lot. All kindsa things about Africa. It was like she was searching for something she didn't think she had.

"I understood it," she said. "In the eighties we was wearin' those leather medallions and listening to Public Enemy. We wanted to be down with the struggle, too. Most black folks have a lil' taste of that in they life. So we ain't try to stop her. We figured it was just a phase."

"That doesn't sound like anything that'd put her in harm's way."

"We are baffled, honey. She started having dreams and hearing voices. We took her to the doctor. We tried everything."

"Do you still have the books she was reading? Did any of them look occultic?"

"She must have took 'em back to where she got 'em, but I didn't see nothing that looked bad. Not a one of them seemed like something we wouldn't want her to fool with. None she brought home."

She sighed, her head cast down. "I told her we was a proud family and all she needed to know about the Jacobses and the Thomases were right here in America. But she got sicker and sicker, and when she couldn't stand to go to church no more, we got worried. Pretty soon anything to do with Jesus would make her fly into a rage. Or make that thing in her go crazy. That wasn't my Milla."

"Did you make sure it wasn't . . ." I hated to say it. Reminded me of Mama. "Schizophrenia?"

"Of course we did. I'ma tell you the truth, Emme. I saw too many things that reminded me of yo' mama."

I must have winced.

"I'm sorry, baby, but it's true. We took her to our pastor for deliverance, and he couldn't help her. He tried, but she only got worse. He started lookin' into things and found out about All Souls. They had a doctor and a psychologist examine her, and . . ." She looked hesitant. "I wished many a day you'd show up and could . . . you know . . . see what's in her."

"Ma. I can't . . . I mean . . . I couldn't even figure out what's wrong with Mama."

"Jamilla believes in you. I do, too. She told me many a night that if I could find you she'd be all right."

I looked stunned. "But, Ma—"

Footsteps shuffling down the stairs stole my sentence. A few moments later, I was looking at Jamilla. A different Jamilla than the one I knew. She had always been fair-skinned. Her father is biracial, so she's got that redbone thing goin' on. Long, sandy-brown hair. Light brown eyes. We use to tease her 'cause her facial features look totally black. Wide nose and thick, beautifully full mouth. Now dark circles put shadows under her eyes. Her fair skin looked ashen, with a sickly gray pallor. A foul smell emanated from her, and I knew it didn't have its source in her personal hygiene. Mama Jacobs didn't play that.

Jamilla managed a weak smile. She croaked out, "Emme." She was so weak, she had to grab the wall to steady herself.

This time, I did cry.

Thirteen

I didn't have much time with Jamilla. Her mother went into the kitchen to let us talk in private. I didn't know how long Jamilla would be herself. If she was anything like my mama, she was unpredictable—be it sick, crazy, or possessed. But for now, she was Jamilla. A very scary version, but my friend was still there and fighting.

She sat across from me on the love seat.

"What happened, girl?" I asked her, trying to take her all in.

"I don't know, Emme."

I stared at her. I had no idea how to approach this. "So you tryna go back to Africa on a sistah?"

Her gaze went to her lap. That wasn't like Milla.

"W'sup, girl?"

"Nothin' wrong with tryna know thyself, Emme."

"Know thyself. Sounds almost like Scripture—but isn't."

"That don't mean it's wrong."

This wasn't an interrogation. I didn't wanna press her and

make her shut down on me. "Your mama said you were going to a bookstore. Gettin' books about Africa."

"Right."

"How you pay for all that, Milla?"

"What?"

"I know how much books cost. They ain't cheap. How did you pay for all those books?"

A soft laugh came from her throat. "My parents ain't even ask me that."

"They don't buy books."

"You right."

I shook my head. "Who is he? And don't even *try* to front."

She lowered her voice. "His name is Asa. Girl, he works at this bookstore I visited. I only planned to check it out one time. I was just curious. So, I went in there, and I liked him because he was good-lookin', girl."

"Too fine, huh?"

"Three, four, five fine, Emme." Her half smile quickly faded. "He's smart. And always dressed in something African. He ain't the kinda brotha you meet around here. He started talking to me about our African roots. He thought one of my parents is white, and I had to school the brotha that we come in all colors."

Oh yeah. Together Milla and me were chocolate and vanilla, salt n' pepper . . . we got it all during school. This was an old story for us.

"So you set him straight. Then what?"

"He taught me stuff. About how we African-American descendants of slaves come from West Africa and how we're connected to the Motherland."

"You knew that."

"But he made me see it all with fresh eyes. You know?"

"But Milla, your family always gave you a strong sense of who you are. Girl, I always envied that about your family. Y'all are tight. Back generations."

"I know, but he was different. In a good way. I couldn't stop myself from wanting to know him and hear more of what he had to say. Girl, how many times could girls like us meet somebody who can teach us anything? These jokers out here don't want nothin' but to get they swerve on."

"Well, you don't get—you know—sick from talking about Africa. What else?"

"He was real into traditional spirituality. The Orishas. Voodun."

"You mean Voodoo?"

She looked sheepish. "Yeah."

I stage-whispered, "You been practicing voodoo and stuff?"

She answered with her own whisper, eyes darting toward the kitchen, probably to see if her mama was standing there. "Naw! I ain't practiced no Voodoo. I only talked to him. I told him I was a Christian. I was tryna witness to him."

I thought about Francis. "Girl! You can't fool with no fine bro's when they all off into voodoo and stuff. What did we always say about missionary dating?'"

"It didn't start off as dating. I never thought it would get that far. And then, you know . . . we got deeper."

"Deeper?"

She looked around. "I can't talk to you with my mama around."

"She can't hear us."

"I can't, Emme."

"Fine. Will you talk to me somewhere else?"

"She ain't gon' let me go nowhere. I don't even go to school now."

"I'll work on it. Okay?"

She sat back into the petals of a huge flower printed on the love seat.

I considered her. "Did you do anything with Asa that could make you sick?"

"I don't know. I can't talk about this right now."

"Milla."

"Not here. Okay?"

"Do they know about him? At all?"

She got quiet for a minute. I didn't press her, but I was losing patience. I wanted to shake that girl. I wasn't gettin' nothin' from her. Finally she breached the silence.

"Remember Antoine?"

I felt my heart drop. I didn't know what she was about to say. Was he dead? Crazy? Was he possessed? In jail? Did he miss me? Was she gonna tell me he still loved me?

"What about him?"

"I kept your secret, Emme. I never told nobody."

Okay, she didn't tell me anything about Antoine per se but saying his name told me all I needed to know about how to deal with this. I stood up. "I gotta go, Milla. I'll be back."

"Don't leave me."

"I ain't gon' leave you, girl."

"You said that before."

"I'm back, Milla. I'm not going nowhere."

"I can't tell them."

"Right." I understood.

She sat staring at her hands folded on her lap, and I couldn't help but trip on how everything changes. But girlfriends are girlfriends. And she never told on me.

"Emme," she said.

"W'sup?"

"I went to church with him one time. It was kinda like a Catholic church, but kinda different, too. It was like a Pentecostal Catholic church with a lot of black and Latino people. I ain't think it would be a problem."

"What kind of Catholic church?"

"I don't know. It was unique. I didn't think it mattered, and I only went one time."

"What was the name of the church, Jamilla?"

"I don't know. It had some long name." She drew her feet up on the love seat. "The dreams started right after that."

"Did you do anything unusual there?"

"I was just there. Watching. How could me going to church cause this? I never messed with his Voodoo or Orishas or nothing. I wouldn't do that."

I got up and sat next to her, ignoring the rotten smell coming from her. "Did you tell them about the dreams? And the voices?"

"I told them that stuff. Just not about Asa." She asked me one more question. A hard one. "Can you see something inside of me? Something bad?"

I couldn't look at her when I answered. I shrugged and shook my head. "No. All I see is my friend. And like your mama said, you're in trouble."

"Will you pray for me?"

"Yeah. I'ma pray. That's how we roll, girl."

I had to get up out of there. I didn't think I could endure another moment looking at her drawn out and hollow enough to host a demon. I said good-bye to her and her mama and took that walk back to All Souls and Francis's house.

Fourteen

I trudged through the projects, down Annapolis, and headed back to the church. I didn't think about somebody seeing me this time. I thought about the things I could see. About the curse that people kept telling me was a gift and about how useless I was, for real.

By the time I made it to the parish house, it was dark. I looked over at All Souls Church and strangely, the door was open. I shot a move and changed direction before I knocked on the door to the house and headed to the church.

I stepped into the quiet building and took the liberty of wandering back to the door of the sanctuary. I'da called out to see if anybody was around, but the quiet soothed my jangled soul, and I knew the sound of my own loud voice would irritate me.

I hadn't been to a Catholic church before. I found it both familiar and strange. It had a pulpit, but it was over to the side and much smaller than the ones I was used to seeing in Pentecostal churches. There was that birdbath-like thing when you first come in, filled with water—but of course, it wasn't a birdbath. And that wasn't regular water in it. It was holy water. I knew that much—if only from the movies—but I never knew what the thing was called.

Fourteen pictures, intricately and beautifully wrought and framed in ornate wood, spread around the walls spanning the length of the sanctuary. They depicted different scenes of Jesus going to the cross and being crucified.

I'd heard of the Stations of the Cross, but never saw them in a church. Why didn't Protestants have that? My mama told me art in the church was a poor man's Bible. Here it was true. All you needed to know about Christ was on those four walls.

I felt a little nervous. Jamilla said she went to a Catholic church, and the next thing she knew she was having dreams and evil voices talkin' to her. I didn't know much of nothin' about the Catholic church, and here I was all up in it. And for what? I couldn't even be sure. A home? Francis? My mama? Jamilla?

God, help me.

I walked the parameters of the sanctuary, stopping to gaze at each of the stations. That didn't seem bad. Thinking about Jesus' death. I pushed past my misgivings and meditated on every one of those pictures—checking my heart and spirit to see if I felt okay about it.

Jesus condemned to death. Receiving His cross. The Lord falling the first time from the burden of carrying it. The black man helping Him hold the cross up. All the way to His death and laying Him in the tomb.

Yeah. Not only did I feel okay. I felt at peace. And I didn't feel peace much.

If Jesus could suffer all that agony, maybe I could fight my battles, and a few other people's, too.

What if I can't help at all?

What if I can?

Maybe Francis was right. How could I lose? Maybe he *could* train me to do something for her. If I worked with them, I could get some skills a sistah could use even after I went on my own. And if nothing else, maybe a proactive approach could keep *me* from the madness—literally.

Oh, Lord.

It was too much to think about, but what other options did I have?

I tried to return my focus to my prayers in this beautiful sanctuary.

All Souls seemed prettier than the churches I grew up in. I was used to any ol' storefront joint. One place I went to actually used to be a bar! It still smelled like beer.

I'd been to a few nondenominational churches in Ann Arbor. Kiki preferred those, even though physically she couldn't make it out of her house anymore. Nothing about the architecture interested or inspired me. They could have been community centers with a cross tacked on the wall behind the altar for good measure. This place made a sistah feel reverent.

I headed to the front row. Sat down on the wooden pew and faced the altar, watching the flickering flames of the votive candles and the soft glow they cast inside the red glass jars.

I silently prayed. *Lord, why is all this junk happening to me? I tried to stay out of Ray's face. I didn't eat too much or ask for much. If I could have, I'd have gone invisible up in that piece.*

And then I heard the sweet voice of the Holy Spirit say to my inner self, *I didn't make you to be invisible.*

Tears stung my eyes. A blanket wrapped around my soul. But my business with God wasn't done.

I wish the demons *I see were invisible. Because it feels like it's too much responsibility. Francis peeped me out. I am just a* girl. *I'm afraid I'm gon' disappoint him, and now Milla and her mama. I don't wanna do that.*

Then God went silent on me.

I thought about Mama. I didn't even bother to ask God again if she was still there like Jamilla was. If she was, she sho' was hiding underneath the voices that came screaming out of her and the way she tore at her own flesh.

He had never answered that one. None of the times I prayed about it.

I heard the sound of footsteps and straightened my back, which had been curved in prayer. I ran my hands through my hair and gave thanks for Penny Pop's generous flat-ironing hookup.

I turned around and saw Francis.

"Hey," he said. His smile was wide like nothing in the world beat seeing me in church.

I said a silent "talk to you later" to God, and stood to greet him. "Hey yourself."

"I was worried about you. I wasn't sure you'd come back. I was sorta mad at myself for letting you get away."

"Nope. Still here." I didn't feel ready to tell him about Jamilla yet. I still needed to think. And pray.

"I'm glad you didn't leave me." He smiled, but his mournful eyes betrayed him. He had bad news. A sistah wanted to burn rubber bustin' up out of there, but those golden eyes? I couldn't resist them. I chilled to get ready to hear the worst.

"W'sup, Francis. What now?"

His face sobered to match his eyes. "I've got some news. Do you want to sit back down?"

"I take my bad news standing up. Makes it easier if I have to take off running."

Again, Mr. Touchy-Feely took my hand. I resisted pulling it away, because I was starting to enjoy it. I waited for the gauntlet to fall.

"No need for you to run, Emme. Just make a little concession. For Father Miguel. No big deal at all."

"So, what is it?"

"He wants proof of your identity before you can stay here, and to do a criminal background check."

Despite my doubts and questions, I had felt the comfort of God's presence in the sanctuary. Now panic washed over me. I could feel my pulse throbbing in my ears. I shook my head wildly. Yanked my hand away from his. "Uh-uh. Can't do it."

He let me go without a fight. "Emme, he said it would only verify whether or not you've committed any crimes."

"I haven't committed any crimes." I marched toward the front of the church with his voice shadowing me.

"He won't turn you in to the foster care system. What would be the point if you only have a month before you age out? He just wants to make sure you're a safe person. He's sick, Emme. He's here alone quite a bit. Sometimes I work a lot—especially at night—and only Mother Nicole is here to look out for him. He's entitled to be cautious."

"Mother Nicole is a tough woman."

"I agree, but . . . " He caught up with me only because I had to stop stepping long enough to open the door. He grabbed my hand. Again.

"Let me go, Francis. Why are you always touching me?"

"I'm sorry. I hold hands with the people I care about. I hold Mother Nicole's hand all the time."

"I'm not Mother Nicole. I don't want you holding my hand." Well, I didn't at that moment.

"No problem, Emme. I won't do it again."

"Look, I can't stay here and let ol' dude get me all messed up."

"Foster care is better than the streets. Think about all the hustlers out there, Emme. You're almost six feet tall and cute as all get-out. You think all the wrong people aren't going to notice you?"

Well, I couldn't speak to that.

"But that's not an issue, 'cause you won't be going into foster care. He owes me. If he hurts you, it'd be like hurting me. He might be nasty, but he ain't tryna do me no serious harm. Will you trust me?"

"He owes you what?"

"It's—"

"Complicated," I said, sighing. "You said that."

I started wondering what the heck was up with him and Father Rivera. How long had they known each other? In light of all the priest scandals in the news, I wondered if Francis knew a bad secret and was using it against Father Rivera.

Dang. I can't be diggin' no blackmailer.

Shoot. How whack was a sistah's thinkin' gon' be? I suspected he was a lil' thug back in the day, but he seemed crazy cool now. Then again, how much did I know about him?

I needed to turn around and get back inside that sanctuary alone to pray some more. But I couldn't do that now that Francis was all over me.

I stepped out the door and sat down on the steps at the entrance to the church and rested my face on my palm. All the fight in me was slipping away. "I don't have my ID, Francis."

He plopped beside me on the steps, sitting much closer than he had to, in my opinion. I started thinking Francis might be diggin' me more than I realized. He acted like it was natural for him to almost sit on my lap.

"Where's your ID, Emme?"

"It's at Kiki's house. In my purse."

"Who's Kiki?"

"She's been like a mama to me. A spiritual mama. I left my purse and jacket and the few clothes I had at her house."

"In Ann Arbor."

"Of course in Ann Arbor."

"I'll take you to go get them. I've got to pick up some equipment in A-square. I was supposed to go this Friday, but I'll call the cat and tell him I'll pick it up tomorrow."

"I can't go over there, Francis."

"Why not?"

"Because. Something went down yesterday. And now our friendship is over. Tell the old man I can't get no ID until my birthday."

He pondered what I said. Then he spoke carefully. "Emme. That's not an option. You have to do the background check or leave."

"I guess I'll leave."

"And I'd have to go with you, and that's not practical for me right now."

"I'm not asking you to go nowhere with me."

"I'm not letting you wander off all willy-nilly. You're not

being reasonable. I'm offering you safety. Food, Emme. If I need to, I'll buy you clothes if you don't want to get your stuff, and even give you money, but you need your ID. Just go back for that."

"I can't."

He sighed like he usually does and raked his hand through his Blacktino curls. "What happened at Kiki's that was so bad you'd give up a safe place to say?"

"There don't seem to be safe places for me in this world."

"Come on now, girl. You're smarter than you're acting."

"More than one way to be unsafe, brotha."

We were gridlocked, and I wasn't moving.

Francis forced a cleansing breath out and relented. "I came here as suspicious as you are. I didn't do well in foster care, either. Some of it was my fault. I was angry with my mother for dying on me. Blah, blah, blah. I ended up here, and he didn't turn *me* in."

He crooked his neck and gave me a sidelong glance. He needed me to do this for real. For all his flexing in the house earlier, the good reverend trumped him. His hands were tied. I could tell.

"Did *you* have to show him some ID?"

He chuckled. "I had to do more than that! But it beat living on the streets. If I hadn't have come here, at the rate I was going, I'd be dead or in prison right now."

I flicked a narrowed suspicious gaze at him.

He sighed. "Yeah, Emme. I spent some time in juvie. I got busted for car theft when I was sixteen. I was a dumb kid, living fast and loose because I hated foster care, God, and for a while my mother—who, in my messed-up mind, abandoned me. Her last wish was for me to come here, and I refused, mostly because I didn't know what I'd be gettin' myself into. But I met Mother Nicole. She was friends with—" He took a deep breath. "She was good friends with Father Miguel. She helped me deal with him." He turned the full gaze of golden-flecked compassion on me. "Why don't you tell me what happened to you?"

I hugged my arms to myself, even though it was warm that evening. The thought of Ray and what he did chilled me. But Francis had shared his war story with me. He deserved at least one of mine.

"Kiki is what you call super-morbidly obese. She's a pretty big girl. Over five hundred pounds. When she got to five hundred, she could hardly walk. She can take two or three steps, and then she has to stop and rest. It's a monster on her knees and joints."

I looked across the parking lot. A couple of kids were playing in front of a house in the projects. Made me happy to see them so abandoned to play. I couldn't remember the last time I had fun.

"I met her about six months ago. I had run away from a foster home because some joker tried to put his hands on me, and I don't mean he tried to beat me. I was at Barnes and Noble that time, and I saw this lady, early in the morning, sitting on one of the chairs reading a book called *The Cloud of Unknowing.* I thought the title sounded interesting, but I didn't want to disturb her. You know how it is. You try to do everything you can so people won't notice you."

"Right."

"But she says something, and I look up from the book of Sonia Sanchez poems I was reading. And she starts talking about the book like she heard me think that or something. I figured maybe she was just nice, and I went over to the chairs and sat by her. We ended up talking for three hours. She told me to come to her house and gave me her address. Later on I walked over there, but check this out."

I could feel my heart race thinking about what happened next.

"I get there and this dude answers the door. Her husband, Ray."

"One of the men who hurt you."

"Did you see that when we prayed?"

"A little. You said his name when you were upset after we left Walgreens, but I figured you'd tell me about him if and when you were ready."

So he wasn't always pushy. Good.

I nodded, and got back to my story. "So I'm at the door and I ask for Kiki, and he takes me upstairs. He asked me how I knew his wife, and I told him I met her at Barnes and Noble. The thing is that was all I said. I didn't say I met her this morning or anything."

I look at Francis, hoping he'd believe what I'd say next. "Bro', I'm serious, I get in her room and she's laid up in this big bed. She knew exactly who I was. Greeted me. Told me to come in and sit down."

"That's nice, Emme. I'm glad you trusted her."

"That I trusted her isn't the tripped-out part. Francis, she hadn't been out of that bed except to go to the bathroom or putter around the upstairs of her house in over a year."

His eyes widened. "Daaaaaaang, girl. Are you tryna tell me she could bilocate?"

"I don't know. But it happened as sure as I'm sitting here with you now."

He narrowed his eyes, brow furrowed. "Maybe you're not sitting here right now." Then he started his *Twilight Zone* theme song imitation.

Cracked me up. "You're stooopid, boy."

"That's an amazing story. But you still didn't tell me what happened at her house that made you jet like you did. I mean, I can imagine. You don't have to go into details if you don't want to."

I stared back at the children for a few moments, wishing God would give me a little rest and some unburdened playtime. Those unforced rhythms of grace Francis read about in the car.

"I went to live with Kiki that same day, and it was cool for a long time. Ray was missing a lot of work tryna take care of her, and their insurance wouldn't pay for her to get treatment or a nurse or nothing. Ray was glad to have my help. Kiki was great. She covered me with prayer the whole time I stayed with her. The system never found out about me. I was able to do housework for her and her husband, and they fed me and gave me sixty dollars a week. I mostly bought books and little personal stuff."

"What happened, Emme?"

"Her man got too familiar. He . . ."

"Put his hands on you, and you don't mean beat you."

I nodded.

"How many times has something like that happened to you?"

"Four."

He shook his head. "Amazing. That's how many I saw when I . . . you know . . . what happened to us in Denny's. I saw four faces, and I knew they were the men who'd hurt you."

"I wish God would show one of us how to prevent that mess from happening. You know? I try to push each incident out of my head. Out of my heart. But they're still there like a big ball of sorrow stuck in my heart. They don't go nowhere, Francis. I don't care what I do."

I'd never admitted to a guy how that stuff affected me. The only person I'd ever opened up to about it had been Kiki. If I thought telling Francis would be a liberating experience, I was out of my mind. It only released more pain.

For a moment I thought I was gonna hyperventilate. My hands started shaking, and to stop them, I buried my face in them. "Oh man. Oh man, oh man, oh man." My whole body started shaking. I tried to hold it in, but even trying to speak my words came out with sobs. I choked out, "I'm sorry."

He put his hand on my shoulder. Whispered, "May I please hold you, Emme? I promise I won't hurt you."

All I could do was nod and let it all out. He pulled me into his arms right there on the front steps of the church and I willingly went to him. I didn't care who was watching.

If I had a raft, I could have floated away on the waters coming from my eyes. And Francis soothed me. Murmured prayers in my ear. Ran his hands through my hair and spoke blessings to me. Told me I was lovely and virtuous and clean in God's sight.

"Chiara, *El dios le bendice y le guarda. Sonrisa del dios en usted y el regalo usted. Mirada del dios usted por completo en la cara y hace que usted prospera.*"

I laughed through the veil of my tears. "What did you just say, you crazy man?"

"I said, 'God bless you and keep you. God smile on you and gift you. God look you full in the face and make you prosper.' At least I think I did. I may have said something crazy or awful to you. I'm still working on my Spanish. Sometimes I learn bad things to pretend I'll say them to Father Miguel when he goes off on me. And of course, sometimes I don't know what the heck I'm saying because I rely too much on Google translator."

A very undignified snort exploded out of me, despite my tears. Francis's gentle voice said, "Can I wipe your tears away?"

I nodded, and his hands came to my face, and his thumbs smoothed my tears away. He had the rough, calloused fingers of a guitar player, and I wanted him to play more music for me. He brushed a stray lock of my hair out of my face, and I liked his touch. He spoke in sweet, soothing tones. "I'll talk to Father Miguel and get him to hold off a few days. We'll get your stuff, Chiara. Kiki's husband won't be putting his hands on you again. I promise you that."

I took a chance and laid my head on his chest, and he rubbed my arms with such gentleness I cried even harder.

"I can't go back there."

"Yes, you can. Don't you miss Kiki?"

"I don't want her to know what happened. It's better if she thinks I just left."

"Come on, Emme. You don't believe she'll think you left for no reason."

"I don't care why she thinks I left, as long as she doesn't think it's the reason it was."

"Did she know about the other guys?"

"Yes."

"You don't think she'll put two and two together?"

"No."

"Why not?"

"I prayed that God would keep it from her."

"The same God who gave her a charism to bilocate to a lost lamb so she could help her?"

"Well, if He did all that, maybe He can make her bilocate over here and bring me my purse instead of me going over there."

I felt the vibrations of Francis's laughter against my cheek. "I'll go with you."

"Don't make me go over there, Francis. Okay?" How could I tell him that even if Kiki did know what was up, the thought of catching so much as a glance at Ray repulsed me.

"We need to get your documents, Emme. I want you to be able to stay here without giving Father Miguel more ammo to pelt you with. Or me, for that matter." He squeezed me. "Don't you want to be with me?"

The way he said it was kinda provocative. "Are we still talking about the same thing? 'Cause the way you all hugged up with a sistah, and now you're talking about . . ."

Francis stiffened. I glanced up to see what he was trippin' about, thinking maybe I was out of line for questioning whether or not he was flirting, when I heard the old man's voice.

"Well, well, well. Don't you two look cozy? I'm beginning to see why it's so important to you for her to stay here, Frank."

I pulled away from Francis's embrace. I got ready to go off on him, for real, then I thought about the Stations of the Cross. I didn't see a single station that said, "Jesus cusses his accusers out." I bit my tongue.

Francis, however, did not. "It's not what you think. She was upset, and I was comforting her."

"I'll bet you were."

Francis stood. Stepped up to the old man. I didn't know if he was gonna smack Father Rivera, or what. He must have paid attention in preschool, because he used his words *and* his inside voice. "I know what we were doing, but even if we had done something wrong, let he who is without sin cast the first stone."

Francis definitely had something on him. And I wasn't diggin' that about him.

The old man didn't flinch. A mocking grin spread across his face. "I came to tell you and the first novice in the holy order of Saint Frank that it's time for dinner."

Francis seemed to soften. "I'm sorry, okay, Father Miguel."

Father Miguel gave him a curt nod. "Shall we?" Same thing Francis said earlier. He reached for my hand, taking me by surprise.

I stammered. "You're tryna to help me up?"

He sighed, and he looked remarkably like Francis when he did it, if you can imagine two people having the same sighing expression. It was weird. I took his hand and let him help me to my feet.

"We cool?" I said.

"We'll see," was his clipped reply.

I wasn't mad at him for that. That worked both ways.

Fifteen

I walked between Father Miguel and Francis, wondering if the grouchy old priest might insult me all the way into the house. Instead, he asked me if there was anything they could do to make me more comfortable.

I wanted to stay, "Stop acting like I'm a pole dancer Francis brought home and treat me with some respect." Instead I rolled with the strained effort he made to be more hospitable, more for Francis's sake than his.

We went inside the bungalow without further incident, and right away I caught the delectable scent of fried chicken, greens, and some kind of pie emanating from Penny Pop's kitchen. My mouth watered so much I almost drooled on myself.

Francis went to wash his hands, and I followed. I thought I'd wait outside the door, but he beckoned me to come in—door open—and promptly splashed me with a spray of water from his drenched hands.

I got him back good, and the only thing that kept us from

Water War I was Penny Pop, who must have heard our giggles and started fussin' from the kitchen.

"Don't y'all be in there playin' 'round. You got to eat my food while it's hot. Now, my fried chicken ain't bad cold, but the rest 'a this stuff'll be hit if you let it get cold. And I can't be warming up food 'cuz folks is playin' when it's time to eat."

"You heard, Penny Pop," I said, flicking a few more droplets in his face.

"I'm gonna get you back," he said, grinning.

"If I stick around that long."

An expression of mock serious appeared on his face. "You don't know the day or the hour when my vengeance will come."

"Then I'll dip in forty-five minutes and miss the day and hour altogether."

We let our noses and appetites lead us to the kitchen, where right away Francis made a big production out of ribbing Penny Pop about her cooking style.

"Sistah Pop, do you have any meaningful concept of cooking without pork? Every time you put on a pot of greens I find some poor sow's foot or other body part floating inside it."

"Boy, that's the food of our ancestors. We couldn't eat the good part of a pig, uhn-uhn. Wasn't no ham or pork chops for lowly slaves. We had to eat *low* on the hog, while them other folks ate *high* on it."

He'd heard that speech before. Francis mouthed the "low on the hog," and "high on the hog" part along with Penny Pop.

She caught him and hit him with a pot holder. "And don'tchu go to telling me you part Latino again. 'Cause they be eating pig, too."

"But Sistah Pop," he said, "I think you be putting ham

hocks and a little bit of drippings in the cold breakfast cereal."

Penny Pop paid him no mind, obviously used to that kind of pre-dinner banter. "Boy, I been cooking since before you was born, and you need to mind yo' bit'ness."

Frances kept their verbal dance going by begging her not to overcook *all* the vegetables. They continued to affectionately rib each other until the old man came in with Mother Nicole and everybody got quiet like he was the breath that blew out all the candles.

Francis, Mother Nicole, and Father Rivera settled down at the dining room table. This room had a more formal air, a white linen tablecloth, and each place set with Martha Stewart precision. The playfulness we shared in the kitchen disappeared, and we ate almost in silence, except Mother Nicole, who made it a point to be nice to me.

"So, Emme where were you staying before you came to us?"

"With my friend, Kiki."

"Is she your age?"

"No. She's closer to your age. She's in her upper forties. She was like a mother to me."

"What happened there?"

"Her husband."

Father Rivera cleared his throat, and Penny Pop bounded in from the kitchen and set a gigantic bowl of peach cobbler in front of me.

She practically wailed, "Lord, have mercy, Jesus Father God! That chile just said her friend's husband tried to molest her."

Father Rivera glared at her. "That isn't what she said. I think you're inferring a lot from two words."

She ignored that. Fanned her big ol' bosom. "I can't ta kind of talk. I gotta feed that baby. Some ol' pervert tryna take advantage of little children. Look at her. Ain't no bigger than a minute. Young enough to be his daughter."

Francis chimed in. "Don't let Emme fool you. She can handle herself."

"Not against no big grown mens." She kept fanning herself as if bad things literally inflamed her. She peered at the cobbler. "Baby, you want some whipped cream with that? Wooooo weee! That thang done got me so upset I ain't even put the whipped cream on. Her husband! Father God, Jesus Lord, have mercy!"

"I'll pass on the whipped cream, thank you."

She tore into Francis. "And don't you go to talking 'bout no complex carbo-high-drates," she said. "That chile don't need to be watching her weight. She ain't got none to watch. She need cobbler, with whipped cream and—"

Francis quipped, "Some drippin's in it."

Everyone at the table laughed. He went on, "Real peaches are a lot better for the soul. And it's a better form of carbohydrate, and they're sweet without being loaded up with white sugar. I'm not tryna have Emme miss no meals. I just want her to be healthy."

A mischievous twinkle appeared in his eyes, and he reached over to take my cobbler! "You don't want this, do you, Emme? You want to be fit for the kingdom, right?" He winked at me.

"Uhn-uhn, boy. You 'bout to see if I can handle myself or not, for real. Quit playin'!"

He pretended to be shocked. "Awww, see. You're turning on me already. Now you gon' get all big and sassy like Penny Pop."

Penny Pop put her hands on her hips and looked outraged.

"Who you callin' big? I ain't big. I'm *substantial.* This here is what you call sturdy. I'm gonna last."

Francis looked her up and down. "Until the diabetes sets in. And the high blood pressure. And God knows what else."

Penny Pop stopped his trash-talking by making a cross with her fingers. "Whooooooaaaa! Boy! Don't you be claimin' that mess for me. You know I go to New Testament Word of Faith Christian Center, and we don't be makin' no negative confessions. I ain't Catholic. I don't go in for no sufferin' for righteousness sake. Don't get me wrong. I ain't mad at y'all, but I can't go wit'cha there. I just got some Catholic *leanings.*"

When she said *leanings* she leaned into Francis's chair, almost toppling him over. "Uhn-uhn. I got the *leanings.* So I'ma rebuke you. I ain't claiming no diabetes."

She leaned her substantial body on him until she made him crack up.

Finally Father Miguel slammed his fork on the table. "Can we just have a quiet dinner? Without comedy or *tragedy*"—he looked at me—"to ruin what little appetite I have left."

Francis straightened up, and Penny Pop moved her substantial self back into the kitchen, hips swingin' side to side, looking unfazed. It felt like a blanket of gloom settled on everyone at the table. I decided to try to break the thick silence that had descended upon us with a crack on Francis. "I'll eat my cobbler if I want to, drippings and all."

"Have it your way, hardheaded girl, but if you want to be like Shadrach, Meshach, and Abednego standing in the fire, you're going to have to give up the King's bread."

"Nobody's trying to throw me in the fire right now. For all the jacked-up things people actually did to me, nobody ever did that. And if you haven't noticed, this ain't bread, but even if it were, it would have been God who blessed me with it. When God blesses me with bread, I roll wit' it. When God blesses with cobbler, I roll wit' it. And if He ever calls me to stand in fire, I'ma roll wit' that, too. To everything there is a season."

Father Rivera raised his water glass. "Spoken like a true spiritual warrior." I shot a look at him, and he had that same twinkle in his eye that Francis often did. Francis, however, must have missed that.

"Don't mock her."

Father Rivera put his glass down. "I'm not mocking your lover, Frank."

"She's *not* my mother," he said, his voice steely, but drenched in sarcasm. "Oh, did I say *mother*? I meant to say she's not my lover. Emme and I are just *friends*, and I'd appreciate it if you stopped implying she's anything else. It's bad form, *padre.*" Francis picked his napkin up from his lap and practically tossed it on the table. "Excuse me." He looked at me. "Emme, I was kidding about the cobbler. Enjoy as much food as you'd like while you're here." I heard the front door to the house close a few seconds later.

Oh no, he wasn't leavin' me alone with Father Grinch. I didn't need bro' to steal my Christmas or anything else.

I snatched up my bowl of cobbler, said, "Excuse me!" and dashed after Francis.

Sixteen

I found Francis sitting in his Camry. He had his black rosary beads in his hand, but he didn't look like he was using them. The motor was running, the air-conditioning was on, but he didn't look like he was actually about to leave. I knocked on the door, and he reached over and opened it for me.

"Can I come in?"

"If you want to."

"Whatcha doin'?"

"Thinking about praying."

I handed him the peach cobbler and got inside. Closed the door behind me. I held out my hand. "Okay, I'll take my cobbler back."

He pulled the bowl closer to him. "What if I wanna keep it? I like cobbler. I don't get to eat it much, and it's smelling good, *chica.*"

"I'll crack you in the head if you try to keep it, that's what. And you're in a weakened state because you didn't finish dinner. You won't even be able to defend yourself."

"But I got this cobbler. I can eat it, get a sugar rush, and take you down."

"Yeah, but that ain't right. You can't hit a girl, so stop playin'." I emphasized my words by putting a stern *don't mess with me* look on my face.

He handed me back my dessert.

I was glad he could joke even though his eyes looked sad. Yet, despite the fact that he had his own secrets, I liked the compassion in his eyes.

"Hey, Francis, you said you were thinking about praying. Do you get points with God for that? I think about praying a lot more than I actually pray, and I could use the points, if you know what I mean."

He stared out the windshield. "I don't know if you get points or not. You'll have to take that up with God. If He says yes, let me know. I think about it more than I do it, too. And I could use all the points with Him I can get myself."

"I'll bet you don't do too badly. You pray seven times a day."

"I must need it more than seven times a day."

I turned my gaze to where he looked into the empty parking lot. The kids I had watched earlier poked in and out of slamming doors. They looked spent. It was cool in the dark now—if you call eighty-five degrees cool.

Francis's voice had the dejected sound of someone who carried a two-ton weight on his shoulders. "You've probably lost all respect for me, now that you've seen Father Miguel and me at war with each other."

"What do you have on him?"

His body language changed before my eyes. He tightened like he had a balled-up fist on the inside. "He doesn't understand me. He doesn't even get me wanting to be a priest. I mean, how hard could that be for him? He *is* a priest."

"You didn't answer my question, but I'll let that pass, like I usually do."

His eyes brightened again. "Hey, you wanna learn to pray the rosary?"

I thought about Jamilla's *Catholic* church. I wasn't sure if I needed to mess with that.

Francis must have read my hesitation wrong. "It's just a method of praying, Emme. You act like I just asked you to draw a pentagram and kill a goat."

I tried to say this delicately. "Um . . . speaking of killing goats . . ."

He stared at me, openmouthed for a moment until he cracked up. "This ought to be interesting. That was a heckuva transition."

"Is there some kind of religion that is like . . . I don't know . . . Catholic, African, and, um . . . Voodoo, all mixed up together?"

"Why?"

"I'm curious."

He ran his hand through that shiny Blacktino hair of his. "Why, Emme Vaughn?"

"Come on, Francis. Tell me. Do you know about anything like that?"

"Santeria is like that. It's an Afro-Caribbean religion, most often practiced in secret, but nowadays people are a little more open with it. They practice it a lot in Latin America, but because of immigration, you can find it in pockets all over, including here in Michigan. I've seen signs of it in Mexican town in Detroit."

"Do people who practice Santeria do stuff that could open you up to demon possession?"

"Yes, Emme. They do. They kinda *like* the experience of possession, but they think of it in a whole different way than we do."

He frowned, narrowing his pretty eyes at me. "Why are you asking about Santeria? If you're thinking of a switch, I don't recommend that religion for you. If you have problems with Catholic doctrine, you're definitely going to be put off by worshipping the African Orishas."

"I'm not thinking of switching. I like being Pentecostal, with maybe a hardly noticeable Catholic *leaning.*" I leaned on him like Penny Pop did, but rather than laugh he slipped his arms around me.

I went all paranoid. That was awfully close, yo. I must have stiffened like a corpse, because after the longest minute in the world, he pulled away. His cocoa-red skin a little more red than usual.

"Okay. Lesson one," he said softly. He placed the rosary in my hand and told me to hold the crucifix. I sat my cobbler between us on the console.

He turned his knees toward me, so the tip of his right knee touched the tip of my left one. I tried not to think about how that affected me. This was a prayer lesson. Innocent. He probably didn't even realize he was touching me. We were in his little car, and it was nothing.

So why did my stomach feel like the attack of the killer butterflies?

He leaned a little in my direction, his scent rushing into my awareness; a fresh and outdoorsy smell, like he'd been chopping wood and doing natural, manly things.

I was so into him, I didn't hear the words he spoke. I knew it was some kind of question because his voice went up at the end. "Huh?"

"Pay attention, Emme," he said like a kid pretending to be a schoolteacher. "Do you know how to do any of it?"

"No. I mean my mama use to do it, but I ain't pay it much mind then, and I think I saw a nun do it on TV recently."

I started saying what I had heard the TV nun say, not only because I remembered some of the words, but because he was so near.

"Our Father who art in heaven,
hallowed be thy name.
Thy kingdom come, Thy will be done
In earth as it is in heaven."

"Good." His eyes brightened. "That's good! But that's not where you begin. Do you remember how the nun started?"

"I think she kissed the crucifix."

"Nice! Lots of people do that, but maybe you should make the sign of the cross first."

"Why?"

"For lots of reasons: to remember Golgotha. For protection against evil. For the grace it gives you."

"Do I make the sign of the cross while I'm holding it?"

"Sure. If that's how you're feelin' it."

"Show me how."

He took my hand in his—fireworks!—then fixed my fingers so that my thumb, index, and middle finger tips were all connected to the crucifix. He tenderly cradled my hand in his, like if he wasn't careful he might break me. He gently lifted my fingers still holding the silver Jesus, showed me the first point of the cross by touching my fingers at my forehead. "In the name of the Father."

I repeated the words. Then he moved my hand and touched my fingers to my abdomen with a blush, carefully avoiding my breast.

"And of the Son."

Again, I repeated after him. This felt like such a righteous, holy thing to do. I forgot about the initial fireworks and became enraptured by what he was teaching me.

He moved my hand from left shoulder to right, "And the Holy Spirit."

He released my hand.

"The sign of the cross is a powerful symbol, Emme. And don't make the mistake of thinking this is a Catholic or Orthodox thing. It's for *all* believers. For centuries, Christians have used it as an ally against evil. St. Cyril of Jerusalem said, 'It is gratuitous because of the poor. Easy because of the weak. A benefit from God, the standard of the faithful, the terror of demons.'"

"Which translated means anybody can do it, and the demons are scared of it."

"You got it."

His gold-speckled eyes took me in and fireworks returned with a bite. What was I supposed to do with that? I was so green when it came to relationships, I wouldn't even know what to do if he tried to kiss me.

"Now you can kiss," he said.

If I wasn't so dark, he could have seen that I had turned ten shades of red. "What?"

"The cross. You can kiss it."

"Oh," I said. I tried to play it off.

His eyes sparkled with mischief. Probably said it like that on purpose to mess with me.

I pressed the crucifix to my lips, still feeling so embarrassed about the kiss comment. I thought as I kissed Jesus how I was gonna have to do a whole lotta kissing Him to get my mind off Francis.

We went all the way through to the Apostles Creed. And then we got to the part I wasn't sure about. The Hail Mary stuff.

Either he saw my discomfort or he anticipated it. "Catholics don't worship her."

"Then what's up with all the Mary stuff?"

"Did Elizabeth, John the Baptist's mother, worship her?"

"No."

"The words right after 'Hail Mary full of grace the Lord is with thee' are hers. It's Luke 1:42, right after John the Baptist worshipped Jesus right in his mother's womb. The Bible tells us Elizabeth said, 'Blessed art thou among women, and blessed is the fruit of thy womb.'" His eyes shone with excitement. "Emme, when we pray that, we're quoting the Scripture."

I couldn't argue with that.

"Nobody is going to try to convert you. Our team is an ecumenical group. It's only a few of us, but we're from all over in our church experience. Mother Nicole is Eastern Orthodox. Father Rivera is Roman Catholic. Dr. Michael Black is Anglican, and Dr. Stormie Jaynes is a Pentecostal. We don't do the same things on Sunday mornings, but we have this in common. We all worship Jesus. We can all say the Creed confidently."

"I still don't know about all this."

"Look, Emme. I'm not the ecumenical poster boy. I'm like you. More than you know. I came to this ministry wanting to have no part of it. Not trusting people who might believe a little differently than me. And definitely not sure about Father Miguel. But I was won over by the love in the group. We're all genuinely concerned about the people we are helping."

I considered that. I'd dealt with demons most of my life, but hadn't actually helped people. Not really.

"Emme, you won't be able to do this work with us if you have some serious issues with me or Father Miguel showing Jesus' mama some love. We don't worship her. At all. But you'll hear her name called in an exorcism—hers and a bunch of other saints. We use the Roman ritual. You'll hear Father Miguel asking a list of saints to intercede for him. It's called the Litany of Saints. He calls on all that's holy, Emme, in a battle against all that's unholy. We use holy water. Blessed salt. Anointed oil. And the prayers of the saints and Jesus' holy mother, Mary. Because she is holy, Emme. To put it in Pentecostal terms, she accepted Christ as her personal savior before anybody else did. You can't be more personal than pregnant with Him. Nobody on Earth received Him more than she did."

"You've got a point."

"The demons can't stand His mama. For obvious reasons."

"Okay. I'll trust you on that. I'm down wit' her, but I ain't gon' worship her."

Again, his laugh that's almost as yummy as Penny Pop's cobbler. "Good. Don't worship anyone but God."

After a few moments I asked what I'd been avoiding thinking about. "Can you get possessed going to a Catholic church?"

He sighed the way he usually does. "Is that a trick question?"

"No."

"You left a Catholic church before dinner. Are you now riddled with demons?"

"No. And don't be all sarcastic. I'm serious."

"Why are you asking me this?"

Jamilla.

"I'm tryna find out more about Catholic stuff. I got the *leanings.*" But I sho' wasn't gon' lean on him again.

He saw right through me like I was made of glass, but didn't press me. "You're a trip, Em. You know that, don't you?"

"My mama used to call me Em."

"Does it bother you?"

The way I shrugged my shoulders was kinda noncommittal. But in truth, it did. Some parts of my mama I wanted to keep between us.

He didn't seem to mind. "How 'bout I call you something else for short?"

"What?"

"I can call you X."

"X?"

"Yeah. That can be short for Exorsistah." And then he cracked up. "It sounds mysterious. Like some spy stuff."

"Or some Nation of Islam stuff. People are gonna think I lost my natural mind and turned into a Pentecostal-Nation-of-Islam-Exorsistah spy with Catholic *leanings.*"

He rewarded me with the laughter that still took my breath away, and I thought, *Yeah. This is cool. I could get with making him laugh. For a long time.*

He ventured to touch my hand. Just a quick rub, and then he

rested his hand on his thigh. "X isn't just short for exorsistah. X is the symbol for a kiss, and it's the Greek letter *Chi*, which was the abbreviated name for Christ in ancient Christian art. Folks got all knotted up when people started saying X-mas. They don't know their history, or they'd see the significance. You're a Christ-girl. His follower. His Emme. So when I call you X, it'll be my way of honoring Christ in you."

"And a way of givin' me a lil' kiss that won't get us in trouble?"

"Yeah. That, too."

God knew we needed to stop talking about kissing. It might help if we got up out of that small space, too.

"Let's go for a walk," I said.

"I got a better idea. Let's go shopping to get you some clothes before the mall closes."

"You sure?"

"I betta. You'll be in my underwear drawer soon, and I'll look up and tomorrow morning you're wearin' my boxer shorts."

"I ain't about to wear your draws, Francis."

"I don't trust you. I'm taking you to get your own draws."

"Can I eat my pork and peach cobbler first?"

He took the spoon and fed me the first bite. Ate right after me without flinching. I started thinking maybe that kiss might happen before I knew it.

Seventeen

Francis decided to take me to Fairlane Town Center. Man, I hadn't been to Fairlane in a minute. It was so weird, shooting down Michigan Avenue to Evergreen, remembering the Michigan Smart Bus—number 200—I used to take when I needed to get away. I could never buy nothing. I rode so I could get away from my mama hearing stuff that wasn't there, and maybe stuff that was. When I had foster parents in Inkster, sometimes they would let me hook up with Jamilla, and we'd catch the bus together. She was always as broke as me, so we dreamed instead of shopped. We'd go through all the department stores, imagining what life was gon' be like once we got older. We sho' didn't see no boyfriend that would lure her into some kind of demon trap, or me not having no boyfriend at all—and not sure I wanted one.

Unless it was someone like Francis. I blushed again, my inside showing itself a traitor.

I watched the scenery fly by while Francis talked up his work as a studio musician. He told me how he spent countless hours in a studio a few miles away. He'd have probably been at the studio now if I wasn't around.

"Don't let me keep you from doin' your stuff, especially if you 'bout to spend hard-earned money on me."

"The studio ain't goin' nowhere. I wanna do this for you."

"Exactly how do you make enough to hook me up so much? I didn't think most musicians made much money."

"I play with more than one band, work like a dog, and I sell beats and studio time and help other artists prepare their demos. And the DJing is tight. You should come to one of my gigs sometime."

"I think I will."

"When you grow up, that is."

I smacked his arm. "Shut up, boy."

He put on some bumpin' music, and I recognized his bass line, even though I hadn't heard anything but what he played for me at the house.

"That's what you were playing earlier!"

"Yeah. Nice with the rest of the arrangement, huh?"

It sho' was. "What's this band?"

"That's The Monk Funk Experience. It's the only Christian band I play with."

"What are the rest?"

"Jazz band. Rock band."

"Which do you like the most?"

"MFE! What else?"

He probably struggled financially more than I thought. I ain't never heard of no Monk Funk Experience, even if they did sound cool.

"I'll just get two cheap outfits. Okay? And I'll pay you back later."

He cracked up and turned on some Jill Scott. "Dang, girl. I let you hear one of my bands and you decide I can't afford you. I know we're whack, but you coulda pretended to like us."

"I do! I . . ." Then I realized he was messing with me. "You are so stupid."

"Let me take care of you."

Brotha caught me by surprise with that one. Ray's face came to my head. He took care of me, all right. No, he wanted me to take care of *him.* Now Francis talkin' the same thing.

"I don't need that," I said softly.

He took a quick look at me and turned his attention back to the road. "Aren't you tired of that outfit?" he said. I was glad he didn't challenge me.

"What do you think?" I said, pretend-pouting. "It's what I had on yesterday. And today. And maybe even tomorrow. But I can deal wit' it."

"You were in my drawers, weren't you?"

I didn't deny it. "You're changin' the subject."

"See! That's why I'm taking you shopping. First you get in my *drawers,* then you'll be in my *draws.*"

We laughed together, then got quiet. Finally he spoke.

"I'm a soldier, Emme. I dig wearing black all the time. But you're a flower. And that's not a bad thing."

"I'm a flower?"

"I'm sure of it."

"I sho' don't feel like no flower. What I am? A dandelion? Something nobody wants in their yard."

"Nah. You're a . . ." He thought for a moment. "You're a black prince pansy. Ever see one of those?"

"You know the names of flowers?"

"I know that one."

The 'black prince' thing got my attention. "I've never seen a black prince pansy."

"They're pretty amazing. Like you. They've got these purple-black flowers, and the center is straight-up golden, Emme. Like a sun inside those black petals. They're dramatic. I don't care what flowers they're next to—calla lilies, roses. Your eyes go right to that dark, sensual beauty."

"I don't feel beautiful, Francis."

"We gon' take care of that."

Somehow, I felt like he was talking about more than shopping for a couple outfits.

We parked in Fairlane's lot and headed into the mall. I thought he might take my hand and go "black prince" on me, and I'd be a big enough pansy to hold hands like a schoolgirl with him. Truth was, I was starting to like his touch, even if it made me a little nervous. I ain't know what to think about him. What to do, or even to feel. I mean dang. We just met!

We entered the mall through Sears. Lord knows I was *not* tryna see the softer side of Sears. I almost threw my hands up and raised the roof when we walked right through it. As if he could read my mind, brotha took me right into Forever 21.

"How did you know I wanna shop here?"

"I pray seven times a day. I'm insightful, girl. Plus, the cats in the bands I play in be complaining about their ladies spending all their money shopping at Forever 21. Those sistahs come to the studio or the gigs wearing those same baby-doll shirts like the one you got on."

"You sure you ain't remembering that 'woman' I remind you of?"

"She wouldn't dress like that."

I ain't wanna think about her. Or what she wore. I needed to chill with that madness.

Even though I enjoyed shopping and was very grateful to Francis, I still felt heavy in my heart—about Francis doing so much for me, but more than that, about Jamilla. I wanted to talk to him about her, without giving up too much info. Yet.

While I was picking out a couple pairs of pants in Forever 21, I asked him a question. "Do you think something could happen if I went to a Santeria church? Just to check it out?"

He sighed. Waited. Sighed again. "Why can't you torture me with questions like, 'Does this make me look fat?' I got to have the sistah about to give me a heart attack because she wants to explore Santeria. If you think you saw some stuff in Walgreens . . ."

"So you think it's dangerous?"

"Emme. I don't want to call a people's religion dangerous. I'm black, and I'm Latino, and both those ethnic groups practice it. Africans created Santeria almost straight off the boat in slave times because they were forced into being Roman Catholic. But I'ma be straight with you. I ain't with that. I take my Christianity orthodox. That's with a little 'o,' not a big 'O' like Mother Nicole is Orthodox."

"What's your point?"

"My point is Santeria ain't orthodox. By its nature, it's not. I don't particularly have a problem with slave religion, Emme. They did the best they could without a whole lot to work with. Some of them found the very essence of Christianity and were saints! *Real* saints! But others . . ."

"What do they do? How can I find out how it works?"

He leaned into the rack. "Emme. I know you're up to something. Don't try to go to a Santeria church. They're usually secretive anyway."

"For real? Secretive how?"

"You only get invited if you're initiated. Plus, they practice divination. There are four hundred or so deities they worship, but sixteen are the big dogs. They *seek* possession by these deities—the Orishas. Those gods, to them, are like the Holy Spirit is to us."

I didn't think Jamilla would ask a strange, and maybe not-so-holy, spirit to possess her. I couldn't imagine it.

Francis went on. "When an Orisha possesses somebody, the person can exhibit . . . powers. Knowledge of the future. Even the attributes of the Orisha that's supposed to be possessing them."

"You mean the way a Christian can, by the Holy Spirit, manifest a Word of knowledge, or speak in tongues, or have the fruit of the Spirit?"

"Yeah. But we ain't talking the same gods as they are. Yo, that thing in the Creed? 'I believe in One God the Father, Maker of heaven and earth, and in His Son Jesus Christ, the only begotten, and in the Holy Spirit, who proceedeth from the Father'? That's what I'm talking about. One God in three persons. The Holy Trinity. Not the Orishas."

We dropped the serious talk as I picked out two outfits with two extra shirts, but he wouldn't have it. He made me buy *seven* complete outfits, and some extra shirts.

We made a quick dash to Victoria's Secret, which he refused to go into. I got some jammies and underwear with the quickness, so I wouldn't have to wear his draws.

When I got out of there he said, "Let's go to Macy's."

"Francis, I got enough. I didn't even have this much stuff at Kiki's house."

"You need kicks."

"Let's go to Footlocker then. We don't have to get kicks at Macy's."

"Stop arguing, girl. Be a pansy."

"Okay, black prince."

He held my bags, and I pelted him with more questions about the *work.* These, he answered graciously. I knew he could tell I was warming up to the idea, so he didn't discourage the questions.

"Do you think if I concentrate really hard I can make something happen with this thing you call my gift?"

He tilted his head and gazed at me, thoughtfully. "I don't know, X. Do *you* think you can?"

I shrugged. "I never tried to on purpose. Seeing demons isn't necessarily fun."

"I can't even imagine, Emme. It's amazing to me."

Francis led me straight to Macy's shoe department. My Timbs were still straight, so I didn't need anything like that. I looked at some Nikes.

"Nope," he said. "No Nikes."

"No sneaks?"

"Not tonight."

So I headed over to the heels. I didn't have a skirt, but maybe he wanted me to get some church shoes or something. "You want me to get dress shoes?"

"Nope," he said.

"What?"

"You better get some diva boots."

I laughed nervously. "What?"

"Kick-butt diva boots. Prada. Stiletto heels."

"I prefer a kitten heel."

"That ain't what you said in Walgreens. I distinctly remember you wished for a heel you could put through a devil's head. Can't do that with no kitten heel. Kitten heels ain't threatening."

"You said I couldn't hurt a demon with high heels."

He grinned at me, "Yeah, but a brotha can dream."

I couldn't help but smile. This fool was about to make my dream come true. "Are you sure?"

"You better hurry. Store closes in ten minutes."

I wrapped my arms around his neck. Oops. Shouldn't have done that. He was more than a little receptive to my burst of joyful appreciation. His arms went to my waist again, and we stood there staring at each other.

I lost my natural mind. I wanted to kiss him with everything in me. I even lifted my face to his to do it, my heart going a gazillion beats a minute. I stopped just short of his lips.

He hadn't moved to meet me.

My face burned with embarrassment. The worse part was I knew he wanted to. I was in his arms, and it was almost like we were praying together. I felt him wanting that kiss the same way I did. Like I had his gift. But he didn't move.

I released him. "Sorry," I said.

"Yeah. Uh. You probably shouldn't do that again."

"You don't have to worry about that."

I swallowed hard. And speaking of Africa. My heart had slowed down, but now it beat like a talking drum, telling me what was developing between Francis and me was going way too fast.

It was as if he read my thoughts.

"We'll just slow our roll. Get your Prada on, so we can get out of here."

Now I felt all weird, like I didn't want to feel obligated to him. "I don't need you buying me anything like this."

"I want to. Go ahead, X. Let's just get the boots and go."

"But maybe I shouldn't . . . I mean . . . you know . . . you've already given me so much."

He softened. "Look, X. Men have never given you a gift without strings—if they've given you any gifts at all. They've done a lot of taking. I really want you to have something you've dreamed of having for a long time. No strings. Just a grand gift—kind of like grace, only with stiletto heels. Really. I want you to have them."

I clutched the boots to me like no one was gonna take 'em now that I got 'em. "Okay."

After he paid for my dream come true, he took up all the shopping bags, suddenly looking very weary. He took a deep breath. "I'm sorry, Emme. I've got a lot on my mind, and I need to get home to pray about some things."

"Yeah, Francis. I need to pray about a few things myself."

Eighteen

After a silent trip home, Francis went to pray. I went to my temporary room and dressed in my modest Victoria's Secret pink pajamas. Poor Francis. He refused to let me show them to him, not even just peeking into the bag.

I slept like an angel on his bed. At least until it was can't-see-in-the-morning early when knocking at my door woke me. It was Mother Nicole. She let herself in. "Morning, sunshine!"

I blinked at her. "It's morning, all right. So early it's still dark outside."

"It's five-thirty, lovie."

"Uh-huh?"

"Time to pray."

"Mother Nicole are you, like, taking prayer requests door-to-door in this house, or did you single me out?"

"No, lovie. I'm not taking requests. Anything you want to talk to God about, you can tell Him yourself."

"The mornin' office. It's not just for nuns, huh?"

"It's for the priesthood of all believers." I couldn't believe how she glowed inside her black habit way before the crack of dawn. "You can consider yourself a neo monastic now."

She smiled, but it was lousy with sarcasm—one of those vicious, Catholic-school-teacher-nun smiles, from the kind of lady who hits you with rulers and makes your life miserable. I thought we were cool.

I pulled the pillow over my head and moaned. "Why do I gotta get up so early, too?" I said, my words muffled by the pillow. I took it off. "I was gonna start working on praying the rosary when I woke up—after the sun came up," I said, hoping she'd take the hint. She didn't.

"This wasn't my idea. Francis said you'd probably want to join us. He seemed to think you had some things you needed to pray about this morning."

Francis had ratted me out. Maybe. Now I was embarrassed. What if she knew I wanted to kiss a brotha I just met Friday? I propped myself up on one arm.

"It's okay, lovie. Francis was upset. I think he needs you to do this. We'll take it slow. I don't want to overwhelm you."

"You overwhelmed me when you came here before dawn," I said, trying to at least get to a sitting position.

Again, that vicious nun smile. Okay, it really is gentle, but still!

"Welcome to my world, lovie. I'm by nature a night person. Add to that I'm up with Miguel at night a lot caring for him. And yet . . ."

"Aw, Mother Nicole!"

"Now you go put on one of those pretty outfits Frankie bought you and meet me right outside this door in exactly ten minutes."

"So he's gon' be there, too?"

She chuckled. "Misery loves company."

I pouted and slogged to the closet and grabbed an outfit. Got my unmentionables from the dresser drawer. I muttered my list of complaints all the way to the bathroom, accompanied by the sound of Mother Nicole's laughter following me down the hall.

Then I smiled. At least one of us wasn't grumpy.

As I approached the bathroom door, Francis popped out looking fresh as a black prince. He sho' didn't look like no pansy. He gave me an apologetic shrug and a shy smile. "Remember, Jesus said we need to pray always and not lose heart."

"Yeah, but He didn't say we had to lose sleep," I said.

"Well, actually, in the Gospels, right before He was crucified—"

"Shut up and get out of the bathroom."

"I guess you're not a morning person."

"It ain't mornin' yet!"

He stepped aside and let me in. I hoped the old folks had it right when they said prayer changes things, 'cause the first thing that needed to change?

My attitude about morning prayer.

I'd dressed in a pair of black button-fly Levi's knockoffs Francis bought me. My royal-blue patterned silk tunic, with an empire waist and three-quarter-length sleeves, had an unmistakably feminine vibe. It even had little black pearl buttons at the cuffs. Although it was new, it had a vintage feel about it. I hadn't worn anything so pretty in a long time, and it helped shake me outta my salty mood. I smiled, thinking of Francis—despite how early it was—because of his thoughtfulness. At least I hoped that's why I was smiling.

The three of us gathered inside All Souls Church, where Father Miguel waited. Had he lit the candles? Or did they stay lit all the time? It was weird, because some were lit and some weren't. *Must be a Catholic thing.*

I don't know what I was expectin', but it wasn't as strange as I'd imagined. Father Rivera kicked us off by praying and kinda chanting what sounded like words from one of the psalms.

"O Lord, open my lips."

Mother Nicole and Francis responded, "And my mouth will proclaim your praise," as Francis handed me a prayer book opened to the correct page. From there I followed Francis's lead.

After a few more call-and-response prayers, I started getting the hang of it. It was kinda like the Pentecostal church. Preacher sings something. You sing it after him. Father Miguel led us, and we responded for a while. Then we got to the Our Father and the Glory Be. I knew those from my rosary lesson. We sang a completely unfamiliar hymn. At Kiki's church—the one she recommended *I* go to, that is—we had been stuck on "I Could Sing of Your Love Forever" forever. Maybe she went via bilocation. She never said.

I sang along with the three of them as best I could. Next Mother Nicole read a Scripture, or rather, kinda chanted it like Father Miguel had done.

All my life I heard that you're supposed to make up your prayers right on the spot. Ones written out for you weren't as good, but those Liturgy of Hours prayers in that book sho' did feel good to me, even if they weren't spontaneous. I could see why people prayed them seven times a day. Their souls had to be as full as the people's who made extemporaneous prayers to God.

When we finished, it seemed like the time had passed too quickly. My mind didn't even wander off—well, it did at first, but only because I was nervous and didn't want to mess up. I definitely didn't fall asleep!

Mother Nicole ended the session with interceding for other people and finally added the benediction, "May the Lord bless us and keep us from all harm; and may He lead us to eternal life."

Amen to that!

By now I felt good and awake, and all holy and righteous to boot. And hungry. We headed over to the house and were greeted by Penny Pop's food. Sistah was throwin' down in the kitchen, again, bacon sizzling. Mother Nicole and Father Rivera took off. Francis came in the kitchen and sat down with me, but he didn't eat.

"Fasting?" I teased.

"It sorta defeats the purpose if you tell people."

"Why you tryna fast? Is this about . . ."

"It's not about last night, Emme. It's about Mass. I'm about to go to church."

"You gotta fast for church?"

"A lot of people fast before communion."

"I thought you said you weren't Catholic. How you gon' take communion?"

"I'm not. Yet. I want to have the discipline down, so it won't be as hard later."

Yeah. Mr. Discipline. Mr. I-Can-Feel-What-You-Feel-Too.

"You're not salty with me for wanting a disciplined spiritual life, are you?"

"Naw," I said. Penny Pop set a plate in front of me. She wasn't talkin' smack today. Must've been too early for her.

"I think what you need to focus on is that discipline doesn't mean 'lacking in desire.'"

"I ain't ask you about your desires," I said.

He sighed. "Are you coming to Mass? It's not Santeria!"

"I'll check it out. What time does it start?"

"Nine thirty. Want to go for a jog after you eat?"

I stopped midway from putting a hot, greasy, porky piece of bacon in my mouth and looked at him, incredulous.

"Of course," he said. "I told you we were gonna get you in top physical form."

"You don't like my form?"

He tried to suppress a grin. "Just because you're *fine* doesn't mean you're in shape. We're not running for you to lose weight. I want you to increase your cardio strength and endurance."

"I gotta pray first thing in the morning, jog, *and* go to Mass, all before noon?"

"I'll let you wear my sweats so you won't get your flower clothes messed up."

"Aren't *you* generous," I quipped.

"You thought so last night."

That kiss that didn't happen flashed in my mind. "Not as much as you think I did."

He harrumphed. Brotha knew *exactly* what I meant.

That exercising thing? I could tell that was gonna be a trip. Francis disappeared into his old—my temporary—bedroom and promptly came back with a pair of his sweats and a T-shirt.

I held them up to get a good look at them. "Think I'll look as good in your clothes as you do?"

That dimple of his peeked at me. "Stop flirting."

"What are *you* doing, bro'? Buying me clothes. Letting me wear yours. Keep it up and I'm gonna end up being your girlfriend. Or you'll be mine. But you can't wear my diva boots. I don't care how big a transvestite you become."

"Cut it out, X, I ain't about to be your *girlfriend.* And yes, I know what option that leaves, but we won't get into that. Right, Chiara?"

"Right," I said.

He hesitated, which told me he wanted to say more about, but wouldn't let himself. And that was probably a good thing.

A real good thing.

~

We started off walking briskly about fifty paces, then jogged fifty more feet, alternating between the two until I built up my endurance enough to jog continuously. We ran a quarter of a mile, then power walked the same distance.

Jogging actually felt good. I wasn't in as good a shape as I wished I were, but I wasn't in as bad shape as I thought I was, either. I think Francis was surprised that I kept up with him.

I worked up a good sweat. Mr. Gorgeous looked like he could easily go another ten miles. And man, did he look good!

When we stopped, he wouldn't let me leave until I stretched, citing that my muscles would thank me for the cooldown later. I didn't want to stretch. I wanted to indulge my muscles in what they immediately wanted to do—cease and desist all exercising.

Francis watched over me to make sure I did the stretches correctly. It wasn't like I never exercised before. I thought he could cut me some slack.

Okay, I knew he was trying to be a good trainer, but he was starting to get on my nerves. After that tiny little hug we shared at the mall, he was avoiding me like I had bird flu. And now, when we finally did interact, he went into "trainer" mode. Yoda Boy must have thought he was some wise sage, so much *older* than me. I knew he was just as young as me, and in a few seriously glaring ways, just as unsure about life.

I started feelin' a little salty with him for real. Like maybe I needed to push him off his high and mighty throne. So, I made a big production out of stretching one of my long legs with the grace and agility of a ballet dancer under his intense watchfulness.

Yeah. Let's see how "professional" he'd act now. I could sense by his getting fidgety that he was feelin' me. Yep, he was a man like all the rest of them.

Shoot. Things flipped on me. When he couldn't hide his appreciative gaze, though he tried to, that started making *me* uncomfortable, and more than a little warm all over. When I started that madness, I hadn't considered how men looking at me made me feel creepy in general. But now I felt—I dunno, something was mixed in with that discomfort. Something womanly, 'cause he sho' wasn't looking at me like I was a little girl. I might be lean, but I knew I had legs for days.

From that stretch I flowed into the splits. I must've blown his mind, 'cause that boy started blinking his eyelids like he was a Viewmaster.

I liked the attention. A lot. Then something clicked in my mind. All of a sudden, thoughts of having some kind of feminine power over him consumed me, followed by a flurry of, like, *thoughts.* I needed a parental advisory sticker slapped on my forehead—my brain was definitely featuring adult content.

I tried to push the thoughts away and ignore what they were doing to my body, but they kept coming back like a mosquito buzzing around my face. Now I felt all paranoid, thinking that every move I made was eliciting some kind of lewd response from him, whether or not it was actually happening. Unrelenting R-rated thoughts assaulted me, until I couldn't handle it anymore.

I got up from the ground. Shame burned so deeply within me I couldn't look at Francis. Those weren't the kind of thoughts I entertained. Most of the time the very thought of—well, *being* with a guy scared me!

Francis stepped up to me. He didn't call me X, thank goodness. It would have had a different, more sinister meaning this time. "Emme, are you okay?"

Having him so close and hearing his voice caused a jolt of lust to surge through me, as if I'd been hit with an electric charge. It was so discomforting I yelled at him without meaning to. "Why?"

"I know what's happening."

Aw, *heck-e-naw*!

"Don't say anything to me, Francis. Leave me alone!"

"It's an attack."

"What kind of attack?"

"It's demonic. They don't want you to do the *work.*"

"I ain't say I was doin' no *work.*"

"I know you went to see Jamilla."

Now I was really annoyed. "How did you know that?"

"I'm not stupid, Chiara. I know you're gonna help because . . . I can feel it. Like I can feel what's happening to us now."

I put my hand up to stop him from coming any closer. "Stay away from me, a'ight?"

He froze, but he had that same look on his face he did when he felt the evil presence come into the Walgreens.

I was even more embarrassed now. Could he pick up on all the bad things I was feeling and thinking about him? I couldn't bear the thought of that. I started backing away from him.

"Emme, hold up! We can pray through this."

But before he could say anything else, I was out.

Nineteen

I didn't go to Mass. Mother Nicole found me about around noon, in the fetal position in the middle of Francis's bed. She knocked on the door, and when I didn't answer she announced she was coming in and did just that. She sat on the bed, being quiet with me for a while, rubbing my back and praying. She kept her prayers simple and true to what you'd imagine a nun would do. She prayed right from the Psalms.

"Have mercy on me, O God, in Your faithful love, in Your great tenderness wipe away my offenses; wash me from guilt, purify me from my sin. For I am well aware of my offenses, my sin is constantly in my mind."

I squeezed my eyes shut, but tears slipped through just the same. Mother Nicole went on, as I sniffled and wept, "Purify me with hyssop till I am clean, wash me till I'm whiter than snow. Let me hear sounds of joy and gladness, and the bones You have crushed will dance."

God knows I didn't feel like I ever wanted to dance again—

or stretch for that matter! I longed to feel the joy and gladness Mother Nicole spoke about, but I only felt disgust in myself, and sadness. I choked back another sob.

Mother Nicole held and comforted me, until I calmed enough for her to get some conversation out of me. "Tell me," she said.

"M-Mother Nicole, I'm a bad person. I had the most evil thoughts."

"What kind of thoughts, lovie?"

"Nasty ones about me and Francis."

"Tell me about them."

I couldn't even say the words.

She took my face in her hands and made me look at her. "Emme. You are a young woman, and he is a young man. You're spending a lot of time with him, and it's obvious that the two of you are attracted to each other. It's natural that a thought would cross your mind now and then."

"It was a lot more than a thought."

She pushed my hair back from my face. "I know it was, Emme. Francis told me all about it."

Okay. I so didn't wanna hear that, even though I knew he probably told her something or she wouldn't have been here. Still, a fresh wave of tears welled in my eyes.

Mother Nicole kept talking to me. "You were attacked, lovie, by the enemy of your soul and all God's people. Both of you were."

I shook my head. "No, it was *me*, Mama Nick."

"Listen, Emme, I need to talk to you some more about the *work.* I know everything is happening very quickly, but there are things we should have warned you about. Things you must be aware of if you're going to do any kind of deliverance work."

She reached into the pocket of her habit. There were surprise pockets that I didn't think would be there, and she pulled a tissue out from one for me to wipe my face and blow my nose with. When I got myself a little more together, she went on. "Frankie suspects you were harassed by demons when you were a small child. Is this true?"

"Yeah." She didn't think I was crazy. I thanked God for that.

She probed gently. "What usually happened when they came to you?"

"They would try to choke me or attack me in my sleep, pinning me to the bed so I couldn't move. I think they wanted to get inside of me, but my mama protected me and covered me with her prayers. She taught me to use the name of Jesus defensively against them. As soon as I'd see them after that, I'd call on Jesus' name and they'd flee."

"So that's about the extent of how they came to you?"

I shrugged my shoulders. "Well, they seem to enjoy coming to me through men, nowadays. But that's another story."

"What I mean is did they ever do any other kind of direct assaults? Did they slam doors or shake your bed? Anything like that?"

"Heck-e-naw!"

"Whew." She fanned herself. "That kind of infestation is hard to nix. Good. Good, for you!" She paused as if the next part was difficult for her to convey to me. "All right, here's what you need to know, lovie. And you can't forget this for a moment. Since demon power was manifested to you at a young age, you were obviously targeted for a reason. I want you to be *more* diligent than most. In fact, I recommend you be hypervigilant in these matters."

The grave expression on her face told me how serious she was.

"Emme, as soon as you do *anything* to invade enemy territory—and in your case, merely thinking about joining us in the *work*—you've upped the ante. You're more dangerous to the kingdom of darkness now. And they've come up against you with a full frontal assault."

"I don't get what you're saying, Mother Nicole. I wasn't attacked today. Those were my own evil thoughts. I wish they were the devil! I wouldn't be feeling so bad if they were."

She shook her head. "I disagree. I think maybe some of them were your own thoughts. An oppressive demonic attack amplifies whatever sinful thoughts you have, and they torment you. You have a natural attraction to Frankie. The enemy can't read your thoughts, but he's been around long enough to know human behavior. Believe me, he's always watching."

I sat up, and she reluctantly released me. "Isn't there some verse that says he's like a lion goin' around lookin' for people he can take out?"

"That's right," Mother Nicole said. "It's in 1 Peter 5 and it says, 'he goes about like a roaring lion, looking for someone he can devour.'"

"Yeah. I can see that in my head. It kinda helps. So the *enemy* is tryna make me think about being with Francis in a . . . well, closer way."

"That's right. It's a step beyond mere temptation. He sent a spirit of lust to buffet you and get your mind off preparing to do that which would result in you helping take his kingdom down."

I considered that. "So, maybe a spirit of lust came to me. Shoot. It was so natural, I hardly noticed it at first."

"But you *did* notice it, and then you did something about it—you fled. Keep in mind some people are so entrenched in their sins that they love them. It's like an alcoholic. Make no mistake about it. An alcoholic loves his alcohol. A good many sinners love their sin."

"Aw man, Mother Nicole. I didn't love what I was feeling. I mean, it was kinda intoxicating at first, but then . . ."

"Demonic oppression is a spiritual force. There are spirits of fear, lust, anxiety, all kinds of things, and these spirits attack the mind."

"But it felt so real."

"Francis told me he shared with you that he has a gift of intuition. You may have noticed it's a particularly powerful charism."

"That's why I can't ever face him again."

Mother Nicole rubbed my arm. "Don't worry. Frankie has been fighting the enemy long enough to have experienced far worse than that. I want to make it clear to you that he was attacked as you were. In the *same way.* Are you hearing what I'm saying, Emme?"

I wasn't sure.

She broke it down for me. "I'm saying that it might be a good idea if the two of you didn't spend so much time alone."

Okay, that made it clear. For once I was glad I was so dark Mother Nicole couldn't see my face flush.

"He wants to honor you as a woman of God. He said it'll be weeks before he can get your long legs out of his mind—and that has nothing to do with demons."

I had to laugh at that. "My bad. I had no business flaunting my legs all in that man's face."

Something else was on my mind. I took a chance and broached the subject with Mother Nicole. "Since we're talking so frank, no pun intended, there's something I want to tell you."

"What is it, lovie?"

"I really like Francis. I mean, I know we haven't known each other that long, and I know about that whole priest thing, but . . ." Then I felt stupid for mentioning it. The brotha said he wanted to be a priest. How plain could he make it that we can't be together?

Mother Nicole took my hand in hers and gave it a little squeeze. "Emme, Frankie is young, and he's lonely. Father Miguel is dying, and you are a lovely young woman who's taken him completely by surprise. He's very confused right now, and I'm going to venture to say that life is probably quite confusing for you, too. I can see why the two of you are drawn to each other. But I can also see how the two of you could be a disaster together."

"I wouldn't do anything to hurt him."

"And he wouldn't do anything to hurt you. Not on purpose. But two confused people? They can accidentally hurt each other. So why don't we focus on getting you settled here. You finally have a safe place to live. That's plenty for you for now. Okay?"

I nodded, but my thoughts were still with what she said about Francis and me hurting each other by mistake. She was right. I didn't have to know a lot about relationships to figure that one out.

I needed to focus on what God wanted me to do here, even more than what Francis, Mother Nicole, or even Jamilla wanted. I didn't have to worry about living on the streets, and that was a huge blessing. Maybe after my birthday, I could deal with whatever I felt for Francis. Maybe by then, I'd actually know what it was.

All I had to do was bide my time for a few weeks, go through demon-hunting school, stave off fierce attacks on my mind, while completely avoiding the man I was attracted to and confused about.

Piece a cake.

I sighed. *God, I'm gonna definitely need those diva boots Francis bought me.*

Today.

Twenty

I didn't see Francis at all for the rest of the day, but sometime that night, he knocked on the bedroom door.

Brotha had kicked it up a notch or twelve and was lookin' so far past too fine he was 'bout twenty-five fine. He had on some kind of silk blend T-shirt, and his uniform black Levi's. He had a baaaaad jacket on over the shirt, and he smelled so good I wanted to taste him.

"Hey," I said. I was glad I hadn't put on my Victoria's Secret pajamas yet. "You look nice."

"Hey yourself," he said, then added, eyes cast down, "you look good, too."

He had a yellow plastic shopping bag in his hand that had the words Hotep Books and the store's address on the bag. He handed it to me. "This is for you. I got it to keep you out of trouble, missy, since we can't hang like we were doing."

"Thanks," I said. "What is this?"

"Books. And a DVD about Santeria. I had to go to this African bookstore in Detroit to get that stuff. They don't necessarily pack the shelves at Borders with these joints."

I was grateful enough, but wasn't no way I was gon' jump and hug him. "You're the best," I said.

"Be good. There's a MacBook Pro on my desk. It has a DVD player on it. And don't be messin' with my music files."

"You just don't want me to see your hoochie-mama pictures."

"I don't have hoochie-mama pictures on my computer. Or in my cookies. None a dat. I prefer—"

"To be a priest," I said.

He nodded, knowing I'd bested him. "Have a good evening, Emme. I'd have invited you to the gig, but . . . you know. The attack thing. And the priest thing, since you brought it up."

"Priests don't go to clubs."

"They do when their Chiara needs diva boots."

Having bested *me*, he turned on his Timbs and swaggered away.

~

I lay on Francis's bed for hours, poring over the books about Santeria. I wasn't no Bible scholar, but right away it looked like to me there was some problems with it. I mean, I was feelin' the slaves wanting to practice their religion without catching a beatdown. I couldn't imagine what it would be like to have Jesus stripped out of my life, and the idea that the people who stole them from their homeland could control them and force a sistah to work and breed was awful.

I would *not* be down with that. From the stuff I read, they worshipped their own gods by all kinda subterfuge. They'd substitute certain saints for their gods. Obatala was apparently the big daddy of the Orishas. He became Our Lady of Mercy to the uninitiated. Orunla became St. Francis of Assisi. I wondered if Francis was up on that one.

There were warrior deities and foundational deities, and they all had stuff they did and were supposed to help you do. From what I could see, practitioners seriously believed they were God. I mean, like I believe Yahweh is God.

I put the books aside and thought for a moment. Some of those Orisha names cropped up in some of the black poetry I read. But how could it not? Most slaves had come from West Africa where Santeria is rooted. I thought about Jamilla—redbone J. The girl everybody in the school thought looked white, even though she didn't really. Salt to my pepper. Heck yeah, she gon' want to know who she is if she grew up with that madness.

And I had to admit, the Santería thing was seducing. Some of what I read reminded me of the Pentecostal church. And then I made that connection again. We are from Africa. A lot of the Pentecostal style of worship—how we get our praise on, how we shout, dance, and get the Holy Ghost—so much of how we worship came straight off the slave ships. And a lot of us didn't even know it. That's what Francis meant when he said he didn't want to slam it. He knew the connections. He saw what drew people to it. And knowing him, he had compassion on them. But he also made it clear he wasn't with that. And if he wasn't with it, he was against it in my book. At least I hoped so.

I decided to go to the computer and check out the DVD. I got up from the bed and went to the little wooden desk, way too small for him, and sat in the chair—also too small for him.

I could barely get comfortable sitting there. So, I did what he probably did and unplugged his MacBook and plopped down on his bed.

I slid the DVD inside and watched his player come up. Man, I was in for an unpleasant surprise. I saw what I read about. And yo, in living color, three dimensions, and with his Bose headphones, that junk was buck wild. Those brothas and sistahs were singing and shouting and eating fire and messin' with chickens. They were drumming and sacrificing animals. I saw some foul stuff on that DVD, and I ain't talking about what they were doing. I mean I saw all kinds of spirits that the film editor probably didn't see.

The music and the praise dancing was giving me a sick, dizzy feeling. Then, yo, they showed a woman who had what they called a "spiritual intrusion." It could have been from natural, preternatural, or nonordinary causes, which sounded to me like the same stuff that any exorcist or deliverance ministry would deal with. Only the word *demon* was never used.

They brought the woman to a priest, and when I looked at the listless, mute, emaciated figure, hair standing all over her head looking a hot mess, I could see. I could smell. My heart pounded, and in my mind, I was taking a walk down a long corridor.

~

I'm walking through the hospital with the orderly. A nice brotha. Big, corn-fed type they like to hire in institutions because they got mad skills for when people get out of hand. I saw a brotha like that give a beatdown to a patient because he was mouthin' off. I didn't think the patient posed a physical threat at all.

This brotha seems nice, though. Asked me when the last time I saw Mama was.

"Last year," I say. I don't tell him why.

I'd been bounced around to a couple of different foster homes. Nobody ever wants to bring me here. They always say junk like, "It doesn't matter, Emme. She can't even respond to you. She won't even know you're there." But it does matter. It always matters.

The brotha says, "I want you to be prepared for what you're going to see." Said something about maybe she isn't like she was the last time I saw her.

He stops at a closed door. It's room 379 B.

"You ready, lil' sis?" he asks. I nod, my mouth gone too dry to speak, my heart beating like a machine gun firing bullets.

He opens the door. And I see someone, but she's not my mama. The only thing that looks like my mama is the caramel color of this . . . this thing's skin. I freeze in the doorway.

"This ain't the right room," I say. "That ain't my mama."

"Abigail Vaughn. Thirty-seven years old."

I can't breathe. The air escapes my lungs like a prisoner. I shake my head. I can't even speak the word. This isn't my mother.

My mother's long hair—even longer than mine—is gone. Patches of bald shine from her scalp between wild tufts of matted hair.

She throws her head back and slams her head against the mattress. It is the only harm she can do to herself in four-point restraints. Her mouth twists into a grimace. I see most of her top teeth are broken.

I want to say, "Noooooooooooooo." But a scream pushes past my halted words and tears out of me.

My mama turns her head. Her wild eyes roll back to the whites and a voice that isn't hers says, "She is ours. Because of you."

I wake up five minutes later on a stretcher in another wing of the hospital.

And then I was back in Francis's room, and the lady on the DVD wasn't my mama, my heart, the person I longed for every single day. I stared at the MacBook's monitor. Images of people turning into lights and colors and animals that, like I said, didn't make the director's cut, flew at me. A sick, twisted feeling clenched my belly. For the first time in my life, seeing demons made me so sick that I had to run out of the room, into the bathroom, and hug the porcelain bowl till I could get myself together.

When I got back to the bedroom, I ejected that DVD out of that computer, plunged it back inside the bag, and put it out of the room so quick you'da thought I was running in fast motion.

I decided I was gon' look at Francis's hoochie-mama pictures.

Actually, I wanted to see if I could find some pictures of him. I needed his calming presence any way I could get it. Truth be told, I was gon' e-mail myself a couple a pictures to my Hotmail account so I could have some whenever I busted up outta there. It give new meaning to "hotmail" for me.

Kiki had a MacBook. It was a little different, but this one was about the same idea. I pulled up his Photo Booth and looked at the pictures he'd taken of himself with his computer. He had a few cute shots, but obviously he wasn't into taking his own picture—which I thought was kinda nice.

He said don't mess with his music files. So I didn't. Instead, I searched around and found his regular picture files. There were a lot of pictures from gigs. Man, that boy was fine. I loved to see an instrument in his hands. From what I could see, he mostly dug the bass. Him handlin' that bass took me right back to being in the music room with him yesterday.

After I looked at about forty pictures, I saw the thumbnail. It had one simple word as the caption underneath. *Madre.* I remembered Penny Pop said *madre* meant mother. I clicked on the picture hoping to see what his mama looked like and got the shock of my life.

The pretty, dark-skinned woman smiling at the camera looked so much like an older version of me I thought I'd be sick. She was hugged up with a little boy, all cocoa-red skin and black, shiny curls. I knew he was my Francis. What I didn't know was why he didn't tell me I looked just like his mama.

Twenty-One

I never did get to sleep that night. I heard Francis come in at about one A.M. It was getting close to the witching hour, according to him, when demon activity was at its peak. I wish somebody had a told that to the demons tryna break me down at midnight.

At first I wasn't gon' say nothing to him, but rage roiled all through my insides, and if I didn't let it out, I felt like I was gon' bust.

I stepped out of the room. He had taken his shoes off and sat on the couch, looking bone weary. I realized how tired I was, too. How little sleep we'd gotten in the last few days. How much had happened.

Did he feel like he'd been blindsided, too? I ain't know, and a part of me ain't even care.

I marched over to the couch and stood over him. He wasn't crazy. Brotha *felt* things. He didn't even try to pretend he didn't know I was spittin' mad.

He didn't speak. Just watched me and waited for me to go off. Slipped his rosary off his neck and started quietly fingering the beads.

How was I 'sposed to go off when he sittin' there praying?

I tried to modify the madness and plunked down next to him.

He shifted on the couch to see me better, I supposed, and watch me more. All the while praying. I knew where he was on the beads. The first, *blessed art thou among women.*

His praying the rosary made me think of that creepy DVD.

"Francis," I said, tryna control my volume.

"What's up, X?"

"That Santeria stuff has a lot in common with the Catholic church."

"You knew that the first time you asked me about it. I told you why. So did the books, if you looked at them."

"I looked," I said. "I read how they do baptisms."

"Did you?"

"Like the Catholic church does 'em. Exorcism and all. But they don't exorcise demons. They say they exorcise the germ of evil in a baby."

"Interesting," he said. "I didn't know that."

"They used the name of the Father, Son, and Holy Ghost to baptize people."

"It's a good counterfeit, X."

"They use the stuff you told me in the car y'all be using in exorcisms. Blessed salt and holy water and oil."

He sighed, still praying. "I would expect some serious similarities. It's a hybrid between Yoruba religions, the Roman Catholic Church; and probably other stuff, like some sorta spicy Caribbean gumbo. Emme, it's made that way."

I kept my voice low because I knew Mother Nicole would be up in a few hours for the morning office, and she deserved her rest.

"So what's the difference?"

"The Creed. The tenants of the faith that has sustained the Church since the days of the Apostles. And I believe in the Creed. I don't mean Oshun when I ask for the prayers of Our Lady of Charity. I mean the mother of Jesus Christ. And I don't *worship* the saints. I don't sacrifice animals when Jesus' blood took care of that. I don't use magic or fetishes, and I don't believe in reincarnation like Santeria practitioners do. I am a Christian. With Catholic *leanings.*" He ventured a smile with that punch line.

"It's too close to the Catholic stuff. It's scary."

"What about how close it is to Pentecostal stuff? And don't tell me you didn't notice."

I ignored his question. "I want to see Jamilla."

"I'll take you to her."

"I have to get her out of the house. She won't talk around her folks."

"Emme, that's gonna be hard."

"I can't get to the bottom of this without talking to her alone. Someplace where if she goes . . . off . . . she won't get hurt or hurt nobody."

"I'll work on it," he says. "What else?"

"What do you mean?"

"What else is bothering you?"

For a few minutes I didn't speak, and he didn't prod. Brotha kept praying the rosary; Hail Marying so much Jesus' mama was gon' be busy all day praying for him alone.

Finally, I couldn't take being quiet no more. "Why did you stop for me? At Walgreens."

He put his rosary back on, and sat back. "Why do you ask?"

"Why stop prayin' now, brotha?"

He didn't answer. "You were right in the front of the store. Soon as I walked in."

"And why didn't you walk past me?"

"I stopped to look at the paper."

"You were looking at the *Ann Arbor News*. I lived in Inkster most of my life. I know people in Inktown read the Detroit papers, not the *Ann Arbor News*."

"I work a lot in Ann Arbor."

I hissed to keep from yelling. "Why did you stop for me?"

"Because you looked like my mother. You saw her picture, didn't you?"

"What kind of freaky thing is that?"

"It's not freaky. I was startled when I saw you. I miss her. So I stopped and stood by you, but you were so busy looking at me, I couldn't really look at how much you looked like her."

"Why didn't you tell me that?"

"And get this wonderful reaction? No, thank you."

"Why did Father Rivera go off when he saw me?"

"Because you look like her."

"Why would that upset him? No, let me answer. I remember something you said. You said your mama left the Church because of your father. You said your father breaks your heart every day. I know you got something on him. Could it be that Father Rivera—the cranky old dude you gotta love-hate thing with—is your father? As in 'daddy,' not priest."

He didn't say anything.

"Was he a freaky priest? Was your mama a teenager he hurt?"

"She was grown. She was young, but not *that* young. They fell in love."

"Why didn't you tell me?"

"We don't advertise it. It's not something to shout on the rooftops."

I shook my head in disgust. "No wonder he couldn't stand me. He probably thought you was tryna play him, bringing home somebody who looks like her."

"I didn't intend to bring you home. That's why I gave you more money than I usually give a street person. When I saw you were hungry, it was like watching her suffer, and I couldn't take that."

"What a Good Samaritan!"

"It may sound bad, but my intentions were good. I do happen to know you aren't her."

"She was the only other person who called you Francis. No wonder everybody was surprised. They shouldn'a been."

"I didn't know we'd end up fighting demons together. I didn't have a plan for you when I saw you, Emme. I certainly didn't expect I'd be asking you here to work with us, and I sho' as heck didn't think I'd end up feeling things for you I *definitely* didn't feel for my mother."

I glared at him. "You're one of the most manipulative people I've ever met."

"And you're one of the most ungrateful people I've ever met."

His words hit me like a slap in the face, but I couldn't let him know. "I'm leaving, bro'. I don't need to do this no more. Find yourself another mama."

He stood up. "Whateva." And walked out of the room, leaving me sitting there on the sofa.

I cried until my eyes swelled shut.

Twenty-Two

Francis came back into the living room and gently scooped me up, holding me like a child. I had no energy or interest in fighting him anymore. I put my arms around his neck and rested my cheek against his neck. Did he hear me crying? Or did his intuition compel him to return?

I must have felt like dead weight, but he was strong to be so wiry. That man, bless his heart, carried me once again. This time into his room, and he laid me on the bed he'd loaned me.

He took a comforter from the closet and spread it over me so I wouldn't even have to move to get under the covers. I burrowed under it, and buried my face in his pillow—so I could keep the scent of his face near me.

Francis left the room for a few moments, then came back with a miniature harp. Brotha pulled a fast one on me. He didn't tell me he could play the harp. But the music he pulled from those strings sounded like something straight out of heaven.

For a moment I was a little scared. The Santería music was

still with me. That music had a transcendent quality too, and watching the tape made me leery of everything. Including this man so into Catholic stuff.

But it sounded so good. And I felt such peace hearing it. I whispered a prayer, "Lead me not into temptation, but deliver me from evil."

If I could have cried some more, I would have, but there weren't any tears left. I just listened to the sweet, soothing sounds of his harp until I slept again.

I wake up and Kiki is standing over me singing the song she loves, "Great Is Thy Faithfulness." *She sounds like CeCe Winans.*

"Kiki," I say. I'm so happy to see her. "You're here!"

"I missed you, Emme." For a large person, her voice is high-pitched like a child's, but more melodic.

"I missed you too, Kiki." For a moment I feel sad. I remember why I left her. But she can read hearts.

"I know what happened, Emme."

"I'm so sorry."

"It wasn't your fault. He's a lost soul. He's forgotten how to love me. Ray can't stand to look at my body."

"But you're beautiful," I say. I get up and go to her and put my arms around her neck and she hugs me back. Her soft body is squishy and warm. She smells like Johnson's baby powder. How could anyone not love her?

Finally I release her. "It's my fault he did it, Kiki."

"Why would you say that?"

"I should have been invisible."

Kiki doesn't engage me in this at all. "God didn't make you to be invisible." She stretches out her arm before me as if she's giving me a gift. My state ID materializes in her hand. "You're going to need this. You have work to do."

"I'm scared. I told Francis I was gonna leave."

"You love these people."

"Not Father Rivera."

"He's a holy man, Emme."

"He's a grumpy old man, and he hates me because I look like Francis's mama."

"It's not you he hates. He doesn't know how to forgive someone."

I shake my head, "He thinks I'm out to seduce his son, and that we're tryna play him. I'm tellin' you, he ain't feelin' me."

"Sit down, Emme."

I sit back on the bed, but she doesn't move to sit next to me.

"If you have eyes, you can see. Many prayers are needed. Pray for the holy man. He's sick, stuck, and needs to set things right before he dies.

"You must convince him to allow you to attend Jamilia's exorcism. Her deliverance will fail if you don't go. Only you will see what the others miss, and if you aren't there, she will surely die."

"But Kiki. He won't let me do it. I'm a girl, he thinks I'm too young, and my experience is whack."

"Make him listen, Emme. You must be there. You have power. Make your mama proud."

"But Kiki—"

She disappears before my eyes.

The sight of Kiki vanishing startled me awake. "Daaaaaang." The dream was so real. I tried to shake the thought of it out of my head.

"What time is it?" I mumbled to myself.

I sat up. Felt for the clock in the dark and turned it toward me; three fifteen A.M.

I got ready to lie back down when the room went cold. Goose bumps rippled my flesh—it had to have dropped down into the forties.

In July?

Aw, shoot.

The first thing that came to mind were the exorcism prayers Francis used in Walgreens. I'd seen a copy of prayers on his desk. He'd written them on a piece of paper in his meticulous, blocked print. So I'd stuck the prayers under my pillow like they were a love note from him.

I snatched them from their hiding place, my heart pounding. I could see my breath in the room. Could Francis feel a demon in the house?

I made the sign of the cross. The first one was a Greek prayer against Malefice—whatever that was—given to him by Mother Nicole.

"*Kryie elesison,*" I spoke into the room. "God, I hope I pronounced that right." I went on. "God, our Lord, King of ages, All-powerful and All-mighty."

A horrid stench curled itself around me, making my stomach revolt. I gagged, tying not to retch. I scanned the room. "I know you're in here. Show yourself!"

I could hear it breathing, a low wheeze, but I couldn't see it.

"You who in Babylon changed into dew the flames of the 'seven times hotter' furnace and protected and saved the three holy children."

At that the bed started shaking.

I had gone through a lot with demons. I saw those electronic items at Walgreens fly off the walls, I've seen all kinda stuff, but as many times as demons had come to me, they never shook my bed. "Okay, Lord," I said toward heaven. "I seriously regret fighting with Francis now. But I'ma still need You to save me, like You did the three holy children."

That demon I had spoken to showed itself as I commanded. Brought a buddy along.

Not an attractive pair, these two. And they could use some basic oral hygiene lessons.

The first one, the bigger of the two, had serious dental issues I didn't think even Lumineers could help. The smaller one needed stock in Breath Rx. Human-*like*, but not human. Thirteen or fourteen feet tall and scaly, with huge feet in need of big-time toenail clipping. Thing One's rotting black teeth oozed with a pus-like substance. It sank its teeth into my skin, causing me to scream like . . . well, like a demon was biting me.

While Thing One demon tore into my flesh, Thing Two tried to get me naked!

Hold up! Don't no preternatural being yank at *my* clothing. I'd just gotten that gear!

The pain of the bite burned like a thousand inoculations all at once. It released its stinging venom into me with such searing intensity, I thought I'd faint.

The pain was so crippling, I dropped the prayer and couldn't think—it was as though the power of words had been wiped from my head. I hollered from the deepest part of my soul, and words I didn't understand poured out.

"Ánima Christi, sanctífica me. Corpus Christi, salva me. Sanguis Christi, inébria me. Aqua láteris Christi, lava me."

This seemed to inflame them even more. Both rose from their haunches and stood to kick the heck out of me. I know they were supposed to be spirit beings, but God knows the pain of them slamming into my rib cage felt real! I cried out again in tongues I did not understand.

"Pássio Christi, confórta me. O bone Iesu, exáudi me.Intra tua vúlnera abscónde me."

Demons didn't like it. I felt my body go airborne until it slammed against Francis's bookshelf. Books crashed to the floor with me. I screamed whatever would come out as loud as I could, my mind praying with all my heart that somebody would hear and come to help.

The door crashed open. Father Rivera stood there, crucifix in his trembling hand, saying the same words in unison with me. *"Et iube me veníre ad te, ut cum Sanctis tuis laudem te in sœcula sœculórum."*

He finished with, "Amen!" Then continued with more prayers in English. He stepped over to me and made the sign of the cross with the crucifix in this hand.

I could see the evil begin to dissolve. It was as if the devils were becoming transparent. The longer Father Rivera prayed, the more they dematerialized.

"Defend us, O Lord, with your Holy Name, from all powers of darkness; protect us with Your holy angels from the attacks of the evil one: and from the malevolent wishes, wicked knowledge and psychic attacks of our brothers and sisters who do his work, either intentionally or through ignorance."

The devil's bodies were next to nothing now.

"They're disappearing," I cried, glad I could speak English again.

Father Rivera said the final prayer. "Help us to refuse and rebuke all evil in Your name."

I did exactly what he said, "I rebuke you, evil spirits, in the name of Jesus!" With a poof they disappeared.

My arms didn't bleed, but weird pockmarks marred the surface that bore no resemblance to human or even animal bite marks. Father Rivera scooped me inside an embrace. "Are you okay, Emme?" His tenderness belied the gruff persona he'd shown me until now.

I couldn't even lie. I shook all over. "No! I'm not okay! They were . . . Oh, God . . . biting and tryna tear my clothes . . . *Oh!*" I grabbed hold of him and wouldn't let go. "Thank you for helping me."

I thought he'd stiffen at my touch, but he held me like I was his own child.

Francis and Mother Nicole came charging into the room. Francies rushed to my side. "Mother Nicole and I went to the church to pray the night watch. I could *feel* Emme was in trouble, so we rushed over. What happened?"

Father Rivera answered. "She was attacked by some powerful devils—not demons. *Devils.*"

When Francis saw my arm, the horror registered on his face. "They did *this*?"

Father Rivera answered. "That and more. They'd have killed her, if I hadn't intervened. And what's worse, this room, this whole house, is blessed. They got through the protective barrier somehow."

Father Miguel released me to Francis's arms. He rubbed my hair and spoke gently to me, his eyes full of anguish. "Aw, Chiara. I'm so sorry. This is all my fault. I shouldn't have gotten you involved in this."

Father Rivera rose to his feet with considerable effort. I could truly see how sick he was. "No, it's not your fault. She *is* gifted. They want to destroy what God has imparted to her. It is a powerful charism. God is with her. When I came in here she was praying in Latin. I doubt that she knows Latin." He looked at me with a raised eyebrow. "You don't speak Latin, do you?"

"No, I don't."

"You prayed the Anima Christi. *Soul of Christ, sancitify me.* Not a word of it in English."

Now that was speaking in unknown tongues, for real!

The priest's frail body began to tremble. He reached for Mother Nicole. "Nikolai, please help. I don't *piensa que puedo hacer esto más.*"

I whispered to Francis, "What did he say?"

"He doesn't think he can do this anymore."

Now the priest spoke to Francis. "I'm exhausted. Care for your girlfriend, *por favor.* Take her into the living room and let her sleep for the rest of the night on the couch."

"Yes, sir."

"Stay with her, Francesco."

"I will."

Father Rivera hooked his arm around Mother Nicole's, and she ushered the ill man back to his bedroom.

Francis helped me up. We grabbed the blanket from the bed. He reached for the lamp on the night table and clicked it on, illuminating the darkened room. "Do you want anything else? Your pajamas or something?" he said absently.

He stopped. Picked up something from the night table. "X, when did you get your state ID from Kiki?"

"What?"

"Here's your state ID. Didn't you say it was in your purse at Kiki's house?"

"You know I did."

"Did you sneak out there or something? W'sup with this?"

I sighed. "No, she came here."

"When?"

"I'll tell you tomorrow. It's been a really long night."

He set my ID back on the night table, helped me get settled downstairs, and got my wound disinfected, even though it didn't appear to be bleeding.

My *boyfriend*, as Father Miguel implied, kept the night vigil praying the *Kyrie eleison* over me. I fell asleep to the sound of his asking, *Kyrie eleison. Christe eleison. Kyrie eleison.*

Lord, have mercy. Christ, have mercy. Lord, have mercy.

Twenty-Three

Unfortunately, there have been too many times in my life when I woke up wishing the stuff happening in my life was only a nightmare. The dull, throbbing pain in my arm told me it was real.

I don't like no devils biting me.

And I had to look a hot mess! Thing Two had ripped the sleeve of my silk shirt, tryna molest me. The torn sleeve hung off my shoulder. As much as I liked that shirt, I was gon' burn it till it turned to ash. I noticed I was now wearing a silver charm the size of a quarter on a chain. It was nice, but not really my thing. And my long hair was standing, lying—and flying—all over my head.

I glanced around the living room. I could smell Penny Pop's cooking coming from the kitchen. Francis sat in the wing-backed chair, dressed in his uniform of black jeans and a black T-shirt. He had his onyx rosary beads in his hand, praying.

From the looks of it, he'd gone through most of the decades already and was making his way back to the cross. I waited, following along in my mind as he softly spoke the words, Hail holy queen, Mother of mercy . . . Then he gave Mary some more mother love.

A few moments later, he kissed the crucifix, and said, "Amen."

"Good morning," I croaked. I didn't have much voice left after the scream-fest last night.

"Hey," he said. "You hungry?"

"No king's bread for me. I'm tryna cut down."

He came to me and sat down on the floor by the sofa. Took my hand in his. "You can eat anything you want to, X. You know this."

"I should fast breakfast, Francis. If I had been doin' that, maybe I could have whupped those things myself."

"You're *not* listening to me, X. No fasting breakfast! After last night, you need sustenance. Eat whatever is put before you. Penny's in there making you a feast, as per Father Miguel's instructions."

I sat up on the sofa and adjusted the cover around my legs. As soon as I was done, I reached for Francis's hand, which got a shy smile out of him, but he held it.

My thoughts turned serious. "I used to think I had at least some power. Last night I dreamed of Kiki, and that's exactly what she said to me. I had power. Then I woke up to a butt-kickin'. They caught me without my boots on!"

"I told you those boots wouldn't help you."

"They could if I'm wearing them with attitude! And even if they couldn't help, at least I would have looked and *felt* fly."

"Those devils must have thought you looked *real* good. Good enough to *eat*! Or worse, if Father Miguel hadn't intervened."

"I'm sorry, Francis."

"You don't have anything to be sorry about. I probably let something in with those books and that DVD. I'm the one who's sorry. So please eat. Let me protect you."

I let go of his hand to pick up the charm hanging around my neck and examine it. I figured the necklace was probably another way for him to protect me. The charm depicted a little man on one side and a cross that was shaped more like a plus sign, with a bunch of letters inscribed on it on the other side. "Did you put this charm on me?"

"Yes, I did, but it's not a charm. It's a jubilee cross."

"What's it for?"

Francis got on his knees and reached for the medal, grazing my fingers as he took it in his hand. Even though we'd been holding hands, I still felt jolts of energy at his touch. He didn't tug on the medal, but I felt the gentle tension as the chain pulled against my neck. He knelt before me as if he were a beggar, the chain between us. So close to me.

"I'll tell you a story about Benedict of Nursia. He was a very holy man, sometimes hated by the people in his own monastic order. They were lazy men who didn't like his strict rule of life. At one point the monks in the order got so mad at him that they poisoned his wine. When he blessed the wine the pitcher shattered like a stone struck it. In the Catholic tradition, if a medal cross of St. Benedict has had exorcism blessings applied to it by a Benedictine priest, it has power over evil, storms, pestilences, and the devil's lesions. I wear it all the time."

"I can't keep this."

"I'll get another one, Chiara. I want you to keep this one. It means a lot to me."

"Why is that?"

"My father gave it to me." He released the medal and let it fall back in place against my chest.

"Francis, you can't give me something that special."

"You're more special to me than *he* is." He sat back down, Indian style this time. Sighed. "Speaking of you being special . . ."

The hitch in my breath and my accelerating heartbeat only served to remind me of how much I wanted him to like me. I didn't know what he'd say. Only what I'd hoped he'd say.

"Chiara, I know we haven't known each other but a few days."

"Right."

"But you have a way of gettin' under a brotha's skin."

I nodded.

"I know you have trouble trusting, and I haven't made that no easier. But I really want you to stay a little while longer. No pressure. Just rest, and be at peace."

"I don't have that kind of time. I'm on a mission now."

He ran his hand through his curls. Looked frustrated as all get-out. "Just hear me out, Emme. The longer I'm around you, the more I see how special you are. You're blessed. And I'm not sure what I should . . . I guess what I'm saying is . . . Emme . . ." He sighed. "I want to . . ."

"What? You're driving me crazy! Just say it."

"I know I said I want to be a priest. And I do, but I was thinking maybe . . ."

Okay, he ain't sayin' what I thought he was gon' say. I said too loudly, "What?"

"I mean, you're here for a reason, right?"

"So I've been told."

"I was thinking that maybe you and I should explore . . . slowly . . . the possibility of—"

Right at that moment Father Rivera burst into the room.

Dang! I mean, I know the man practically saved my life. But a sistah needed to hear what Francis had to say! Then again, I didn't know if hookin' up was what Francis had in mind or not. God only knows. He might have asked me to be his prayer partner or something.

I was glad to see Father Rivera looking a little more rested and energetic. "Ah. I see you're up! *Buenos días*, Emme."

"Good morning, sir. If it's still morning."

"Close enough," he said. Suddenly his Spanish accent sounded so cute to me. I was gonna have to ask Francis to teach me some words so I could use a little ghetto Spanglish myself.

Father Rivera sat on the wing-backed chair. I guess his presence made Francis uncomfortable. He got up from the floor and sat in the reclining chair opposite the priest.

We sat there in awkward silence for a few moments until Father Rivera blurted, "Emme?"

"Yes, Father Rivera?"

"Tell me. Who is the fat lady who appeared in my dream and told me you were going to save Jamilla's life?"

Twenty-Four

Apparently I was gonna need all the prayer lessons I could get. Stuff was startin' to jump so fast at the All Souls parish house that only the strong would survive. And I didn't mean strong in body, though that could help as well, as the three holy children in the "seven times hotter" furnace could attest to.

Francis just sat there, no doubt trippin' about what Father Rivera asked me.

I didn't know how the old man would take Kiki, and he had offended me to boot calling her fat.

"Look, I know she's a big girl, but I don't appreciate you calling her fat like that."

He looked at me like I was insane. "Fat? The woman must have weighed six hundred pounds. She was enormous. How could anybody get that size and be sensitive about being called fat?"

I made my indignation clear through my raised voice. "Five hundred and ten! And she *is* sensitive, a'ight! She's got her faults, but I don't know a person more prayerful than Kiki. She can't walk but a few feet anymore, so she lies in bed interceding for everybody."

"Who is this woman?"

"Her name is Kiki Banner. She's the one I stayed with before I came here." I know I sounded like a petulant child, but I couldn't help it. "She kept me off the street. For almost a year, she covered me in prayer, and I didn't have to worry about anything. And she was there for me. All I had to do was take care of her, cook, help her get to the bathroom."

"And what was she doing in my dream saying you were going to save Jamilla's life?"

"I don't know how she got in your dream. She was in mine, too. In my dream she told me she knew I was going to need my ID. Next thing I know, Francis is picking it up off the night table. I had left it at her house when I had to leave . . . suddenly."

Father Rivera slowly shook his head. "Amazing."

Francis repeated, "Amazing!" I looked at him. I couldn't believe how alike they really were.

Father Rivera's voice snapped me out of my reverie. "I haven't heard of anyone with that charism since Blessed *Padre* Pio was alive. She must be a saint."

"She is in my book. She isn't perfect—"

"The saints weren't perfect. They were pure of heart. There's a difference. What else did she say? How is Jamilla's life threatened?"

"I don't know. She didn't tell me."

"I need something better than that. Otherwise, why did she go through the trouble?"

I looked at Francis. He was not smiling. I had a distinct feeling that somehow he knew I hadn't disclosed everything I dreamed. If he did, he didn't say a word.

He'd only end up on my case about it later. I went ahead and 'fessed up. "She said I have to be at the exorcism."

Father Rivera rolled his eyes. "Why?"

"I'm 'sposed to see something everybody else is gon' miss. And whatever it is, is gonna kill her if I'm not there."

Father Rivera stood. "You have no reason to be at an exorcism. You won't provide physical strength. You are not a medical doctor. You are not a monastic in ceaseless prayer who I would trust with my very life. You will not be there, Emme. The dream didn't impress me *that* much."

Penny Pop sashayed in, hips swinging from side to side. "Come on in this kitchen," her trumpet voice blasted. "Chile, I made you my demon-bustin' brunch. I'ma put so much meat on yo' ribs today, the devil try to touch you, he gon' put his hands on solid muscle. And we going let the good priest bless the food today. We ain't takin' no chances. Can't let the devil do whatever he wanna do. We gon' fight back, and fight dirty."

Now Francis got up. "Fight back and fight dirty sounds like a plan, Penny Pop," he said, but he looked right at me.

I hear you, bro'.

Twenty-Five

We ate the king's bread and much, much more. Penny Pop put her foot, ankle, and part of her leg in the food this time. We all ate heartily, and Penny Pop even joined us, but a somber mood pervaded the table.

Francis didn't say much to me while we ate, which worried me. He almost always went out of his way to make me feel safe.

I didn't feel so safe.

After our brunch, Mother Nicole and I collected dishes. We insisted on Penny Pop resting after making such a lavish spread.

"Why don't you go sleep in Frankie's room, Penny Pop?" I teased.

That trumpet voice sounded and nearly blew Mother Nicole's hair covering off. "Chiiiiiile, my mama told me before I could even get a whiff a boys, 'Don't be layin' down wit' the devil.' I know that ain't what she meant, but I can't be up in there with no eeen-que-bye! I be done said *bye.* Devil tryna take yo' clothes off. Mercy Jesus Father God glory! I can't take it. Lord a mercy,

Father Jesus Holy Ghost!" After all that she spoke in tongues. I think. *"Hiyayayayayaya!"*

She stopped abruptly. Suddenly looked at us. "You want me to make you a 7UP cake? I need ta bake. Y'all 'bout to wear out my nerves dealing with devils and eeen-que-byes and such. Who ever heard a such a thang?"

"I don't want a 7UP cake, Penny Pop. I gotta work off all the calories in the spread you just served. You go lie down on the sofa, then. We not gon' let no incubi get you."

Her hips, working as hard as pistons in an automobile, carried her hefty body into the living room. All the while she walked she was praying in that wacky way of hers. "Woooooooo! Mercy Jesus Glory Father God, You got to help us! We can't have no demons tryna take the babies' clothes . . . Lord! Father Holy Ghost Spirit of God Jesus, mercy!"

Mother Nicole and I looked at each other and laughed.

"She's a live one, isn't she?" Mama Nick's pragmatic voice was in stark contrast to Penny Pop's, yet her hazel eyes shone with admiration for her.

"She sho' is, Mother Nicole. I'm gonna miss her when I'm gone."

Francis came from behind me. "Maybe you won't go."

I didn't know what to say. Francis took the dish towel and plate Mother Nicole was holding in her hand. "You rest too, Mama Nick. You kept the night watch in prayer last night. Go get some sleep. I got this. If Father Miguel needs anything, I'll hook him up."

She flicked a "look" at him. Mama Nick didn't miss nothing. She knew he was tryna get some time with me.

He answered her look with a guilty grin. "I got this, ma," he said.

"I'm sure you do, lovie."

I filled the sink with soapy water. Francis worked quietly beside me, as if he wasn't gonna start running his mouth.

I broke the ice to help him out. "You play the harp beautifully."

"Thank you, X." He didn't mince words about anything else. "The exorcism is in about two weeks. You in, or no?"

"Your daddy said no."

"What do you say?"

"I say that doesn't give you much time to train me."

"Or much time to pray."

I stopped washing dishes for a moment. Took a deep breath. Got real. "I've never known Kiki to be wrong. Not when she's comin' this hard. Not when somebody's life is at stake."

"So are you in?"

I sighed like him and his daddy. "I'm in. Teach me everything you know."

"Wear your kick-butt boots," he said.

I ended up doing all the dishes. I didn't see him again that day.

Twenty-Six

The next morning I jumped on the number 200 bus to Detroit and deposited myself on Woodward Avenue. I wasted no time hustling myself down the street to Hotep Books.

It was like every other black bookstore I'd ever seen. Not quite as good as the Shrine of the Black Madonna, but holdin' it down.

I browsed the racks, seeing everything except for what, or who, I wanted to see. A cinnamon-brown–skinned woman with a big Pam Grier as Foxy Brown Fro asked me if I needed help. I took a risk and went for what my instincts told me. "Is Asa working today?"

"He's in the back. I'll get him."

I'm not sure what I expected when I saw him. Francis kinda spoiled me with the fineness, so he had to bring it to compete with him. This brotha stepped out of the back room, or wherever he was, lookin' like the finest thing God ever made.

I blinked. And blinked again. *What in the world?*

Naw, he wasn't of this world. Bro' looked like he stepped out of the heavenlies. Dark brown honey–colored, with a face chiseled like a master sculpture made him. Tall as Francis, but with more meat on him. Muscles that made you wanna grab him. And he wasn't some lil' kid. He had to be older than Francis. I know Jamilla had to know that. He was way too much man.

His eyes flickered over me. In *that* way. "Hotep," he said.

I knew that meant peace. "Hey," I said. I may have known it meant peace, but I'd just say peace if that's what I wanted to say. I wasn't sure I came in peace. "Are you Asa?"

"I am. Do I know you, sistah?" He eased closer, and his scent, unlike anything I'd ever smelled, filled me. Almost made my toes curl in my diva boots, in a good way!

"Somebody told me you're the brother to talk to about . . ." I had to say this carefully. Santeria was a secret society. "African spirituality."

His beautiful face looked pleased. Opened like a flower. I thought about Francis. Black prince pansy. And I didn't see no pansy in Asa.

He gestured with a jerk of his head toward one of the aisles, and took me right to a "spirituality" section.

"Anything specific?" he asked.

"I'm curious. I like the Roman Catholic Church, but I want something a little more expressive."

He didn't flinch. Acted like I came in just for him. "Have you studied Yoruba culture?"

"A little."

"You might like Santeria."

When he said the word, I felt my bones turn liquid. As much

as I was feelin' Francis, this bro' made it an effort to remember Francis's name.

He leaned against the shelf hovering over me, drawing me in like the proverbial moth to the flame. For real.

I cleared my throat to clear my head. "I heard that was kinda secretive. I need a place I can practice my spirituality boldly. You know?"

He said, "Ummmmmm," like he moaned it. It wasn't like somebody saying, "Hmmm." Like when they think. This was way different. That *ummmmmm* vibrated through me, and it felt like I had never heard such a compelling sound. Not even in Francis's music.

Lord, what the heck is going on?

A half smile, bright as movie star's, crept across his face. "How old are you, Miss . . ."

"Emme Vaughn." I found myself saying, "I'm old enough to handle whatever you recommend."

I had to check Emme Vaughn.

Wait just one minute here, sistah.

"And what will your man think about your sudden interest in whatever I recommend?" he asked.

"I'm a solo artist."

You're a what, girl? But I couldn't help myself.

"Do you ever consider *collaborating*?" he asked smooth as silk.

"Depends on how *good* the other artist is," some evil thing said in my voice.

What? Emme have you lost your mind?

"You must be *good* yourself."

"I can be *bad*, too."

Okay. I needed to wash my mouth out with . . . holy water.

He put his hands on a Santeria book. Didn't pull it off the

shelf. "I think I've got what you're looking for, but it's not for babies."

"I'm not a baby."

"Good." He put his face near mine. "We'll need to talk somewhere private. Are you free for dinner sometime?"

Bro' had me mesmerized. Jamilla was toast, if she even tried to mess with him. I was getting singed around the edges, and I came in with a plan.

"Jesus," I said. I don't even know why I called on the Lord, but his veneer cracked. One tiny twitch. A hint of a smile. Then the Ray-Bans came off my eyes.

I didn't see nothin' but beautiful. If I thought his body was fine, with the blinders off, he got downright brilliant.

"Holy God, Holy Mighty, Holy Immortal," slipped out of my mouth, and Asa turned into something made out of light.

"Jesus," I whispered.

"Yes," he said.

"I ain't talkin' to you," I wanted to say, but my voice left. A force pushed me to my knees. I heard music inside of me. Energy unlike anything I'd ever experienced surged in me. I didn't mess with drugs, but this had to be what it was to be high. I couldn't speak so I thought, *Jesus, help me.*

Asa took my hand, and it was like every infatuation I'd ever felt. Vibrant. Alive. Consuming. He lifted me from my knees. Caressed my hand.

I heard a bell. The sound crashed in my ear destroying the peace—the hotep—I felt. The noise opened my throat enough to fight whatever was taking me over.

"The blood of Jesus is against you," I said. "I plead the blood of Jesus."

All of a sudden, I saw a legion of faces shimmer inside Asa's, like images of light projected onto a glittering blank white screen.

Someone touched my arm. "Chiara" broke through the light.

I snapped to attention. "Francis?"

He frowned. "Are you okay?"

I looked around. "Where is Asa?"

"Who?"

"Asa. The brotha I was talking to."

"I didn't see no brotha. But I felt something. And it wasn't a man."

I pulled away from Francis, looking for Foxy Brown. An older African-American woman appeared and asked if I needed help.

"I'm looking for Asa." A wave of nausea hit me.

"He's not working today."

"But I just saw him. The woman with the Afro went in the back and got him for me."

"Honey, Asa won't be in till tomorrow. I'm the only person working in the store today."

I looked at Francis.

"It's time to go, Emme," he said.

Twenty-Seven

I wanted him to fuss, but everything Francis said in the car on the way back to Detroit was calculated and quiet.

"How did you know I was there?" I asked.

"You were gonna be at Jamilla's or at our house. Until I saw the bag in the room on my desk. I know you MapQuested the directions. Where else would you be? What were you doing?"

"I wanted to see the bookstore."

"*Whole* truth, please."

"Whoever Asa is, he's the reason she's possessed."

He stared out the windshield. Scowled at traffic. "The Asa who the employee said wasn't there."

"You felt something."

"From the time I discovered the MapQuest directions, I burned rubber gettin' to you, girl. What is goin' on?"

"I think I saw my first angel of light."

His head whirled around. "Angel of light, like, in a *bad* way?"

"The Bible doesn't talk about them in a good way! Francis, he was magnificent. I don't know what he did. Maybe he bilocated. Maybe he was there in essence or something. I can't even explain it, but whatever it was that happened in that store blew my ever-lovin' mind."

"I didn't see anybody. I just felt you were . . . not yourself."

"Francis, that thing, whatever it was, forced me to my knees. It was like it tried to make me worship it."

"And you think he, or it, had something to do with Jamilla?"

"You gotta bring her to me. I need to know exactly what she did with him. Because if he put on her what he put on me, she ain't have a chance."

"I'll bring her," he said, grimly.

True to his word, Francis, by some miraculous favor, brought Jamilla to his house. We knew exactly when Mother Nicole would be praying. The Liturgy of Hours was how she kept time. *Vigils* is the night watch. *Lauds* are prayers around breakfast time. *Prime* is just before you start the workday, and *Terce* is like a midmorning prayer break. Then there's a kinda meditation-like time at about lunch hour called *Sext.* It's like a boost to help you finish your day. As the shadows lengthen, urging you toward evening, there's *None*, and *Vespers* is the evening celebration. *Compline* is the now I lay me down to sleep prayers.

Francis smuggled her into the house during *Sext*, while Penny Pop was busy fixin' lunch. We hid her in his room.

"Let me talk to her alone," I said.

"You can't."

"I have to."

"Emme, no."

"She won't talk if you're around."

"It could be dangerous."

"Then pray and listen, and do that thing you do."

He hesitated.

"Please."

He crossed his arms defensively. "I'm gon' be right by this door. Praying. And doin' that thing I do. You better hope this works."

I didn't even bother to respond.

I shut the door and looked at her. The dark circles were darker. Her skin chalky and dull. She still stank. She sat on the chair, and I was glad because I could disinfect a chair more easily than a delicate quilt. I felt unreasonably angry and disgusted at her. "Does Asa work at Hotep?"

"How did you—"

"Did you sleep with him?"

She looked down at her hands.

I sighed. "Did you have sex with Asa?"

She shook her head. "I just kissed him."

"You're lying!"

"I'm not. Or if I did do that, I don't remember."

"Aw man, Milla. I can't believe you didn't tell anybody that. He could have drugged you. Shoot. He *is* a drug."

"I'm sorry."

I paced the room. Wild-minded and full of rage. "He didn't take you to a Catholic church, did he?"

More silence.

"You better talk to me, Milla. How am I 'sposed to fight for you, when you ain't even straight with me?" I started talkin' to myself. "We ain't goin' out like that. You are not gon' be the one drooling in a corner of the crazy house. And I sho' ain't gon' put you in the ground because you let the enemy take you out."

I got in Jamilla's face. "I'm 'bout to set it off in the devil's kingdom for you, and if you ain't for me, you're against me. So, spill it!"

"I don't know what kind of church—"

"You're lying. You can't even get inside a Santeria service without being initiated. That's why you couldn't give me a name. It's some kind of secret society. And I'm sure, if you've only seen a Catholic church service in a movie, you had to know when they sacrificed Toto on the altar you weren't in Kansas anymore."

Tears streamed down her face.

"*What* the heck is he, Milla!"

"He's a man, but he's got powers."

"I noticed."

"He's a god, Emme. An elevated man. You never told me about a demon like him. You said they be ugly. He ain't ugly."

"*I* ain't never seen a demon like that!" I yelled. "It was a whole different kind of evil. A beautiful evil, full of promises and hope for . . . what? You don't even know. And if you slept with him, he may have deposited something in you. I don't know. It's too deep for me. How am I supposed to help you? I don't know what to do with something that . . . I don't even have a word for."

"Pure," she offered shyly.

"Pure evil," I said.

I yanked open the bedroom door and asked Francis to take her home.

I spent the night on the floor of the church, crying out to God.

Twenty-Eight

Francis filled the next two and a half weeks with spiritual boot camp. I didn't have to worry about spending time alone with Francis. For all practical purposes I *was* alone whenever I was with him.

He found replacements for all his gigs and cut out the studio time. Our day began with a quick shower followed by the morning office—the first of the seven canonical hours. I kept time to the rhythms of "seven times a day do I praise Thee." Matins, Prime, Terce, Sext, None, Vespers, and Compline. And all kind of prayer from the rosary to the Jesus Prayer in between. Father Rivera prayed with us if his health allowed. Mother Nicole, Francis, and I gathered in the All Souls Sanctuary for every office—without fail.

I missed the easy way Francis and I kicked it when we first met, but now my soul had wings and soared. I hadn't even felt that good living with Kiki. I guess because with her my spirituality had been passive. Now I actively participated in my spiritual growth.

On Sunday, even when he didn't feel well, Father Rivera celebrated mass. Francis and I couldn't share communion with the All Souls folks. On those days we prayed a special prayer together to receive Christ and ask him to stay and dwell within us always.

Francis and Mother Nicole went through the entire Psalter. Both of them had it memorized. I was so gonna memorize the Psalms too, when all this was over.

Late at night I studied for my GED. Mother Nicole helped if Father Rivera didn't need her. One particularly bad night, she had to take him to the emergency room. I didn't have much left to review, but math was harder for a right-brained poet-girl like me. Francis paced around that night, nervous and agitated. Probably afraid. He stayed away from me until about midnight. Then he knocked on the bedroom door flexing his brave front like I'd buy it.

"Need help with the math?"

I didn't have the heart to turn him down. "You feel like it?"

"I'm straight."

"Do you know what you're doing?"

He sat down on the bed while I sat at the desk. Picked up my GED preparation manual and flipped through the math section. "I was smart in school. I quit because my mother died. I was practically a math whiz, Chiara."

He hadn't called me Chiara since the morning I told him about what could happen with Jamilla. I thought I'd tease him about it. "So, I'm Chiara again, huh, Francesco?"

His head snapped up. *"Francesco?"*

"You didn't think I wouldn't Google Chiara, did you?"

"So how did you find out who she is?"

"Took a minute. It sounds kinda like key-air-ruh. I got a friend named Kiera, so I'd spelled yours wrong. I tried looking in Spanish dictionaries. All kinds of stuff. Then finally I got the spelling right. One day I found a singer named Francesca Chiara, and then I remembered the night the devils attacked me. Your father said, "Take care of your girlfriend, *Francesco.* I Googled Francesco and Chiara after that, and who did I find? Saint Francis of Assisi, also known by his Italian name Francesco, and Clare of Assisi, also known by her Italian name, Chiara."

He threw his hands up in mock surrender. "You got me."

"He was like a father to her. Is that what you want for us?"

"Some people believe he was in love with her. Or at the very least, he was tempted by her."

"He honored her. He hardly even spent time with her."

"I understand why."

He lay back on the bed. Put the book on his chest. Finally, he said, "The first time I called you that was in Walgreens. Do you remember?"

"Of course I do."

"I think at that time I wanted a friend. Somebody I could share the things of the Spirit with. No, I didn't want to be a father to you. I wanted to be a holy friend."

"Now you are. Are you happy?"

"I got more than a holy friend, Chiara."

I lay my pencil down and turned toward him in my chair. "Did you get a spiritual daughter?"

"Nah. You're too hardheaded for that."

"Do tell."

He leaned on one elbow. "Chiara was very beautiful. All the

Poor Clares were when the order started. A lot of them came from noble families."

"Your point?"

"Maybe my point is I think you're *fine.*"

I laughed. "I guessed that."

"Maybe I called you Chiara because I thought it was safer. That if I thought of you as this holy, spiritual friend, I wouldn't let lust get the better of me."

"That must have worked for you."

"I didn't say that."

"You've always been a gentleman."

"That doesn't mean I haven't had an errant thought."

"So what did you do about that thought?"

He turned over to face me, propping his cheek on one palm. "I talked to a certain priest about it."

"No wonder he treated me like I was the whore of Babylon."

"I'm no virgin, Emme. Those barbs you think were aimed at you were for me. All of them. He was trying, in his own way, to keep me from making the mistakes he made. I mean, at first he was salty with me about bringing you home. He thought I was messin' with his head bringing someone who looks like Mama home. That was hard for him. He had it in his head that I wanted to remind him of what he missed. But it was never that."

"What *was* it, Francesco? Because I'm not sure what you want from me. You say one thing, then another. You *say* one thing and *do* another."

He rolled back over and stared at the ceiling. "To be honest, I want *everything.* I wanna be a priest who has a woman."

"Mother Nicole says Orthodox priests have families. Protestant ministers have families."

"I've had this conversation a million times with Mama Nick. Emme, the Roman Church is my heritage. She's my *mother*—mother church. I have to embrace her."

"But what about the things you said about creating something new in deliverance ministry? You think Rome is gonna allow an exorsistah?"

This time he sat up, probably ready to rumble because I'd put him on the spot. He couldn't retreat inside his head because my questions kept challenging him. "Come on, Emme. It's not like you even want to be that. All you did was resist until you thought Jamilla's life was in danger."

"That's not true. I got busy as soon as I knew she was involved."

"And if it hadn't been Jamilla?"

I gave him that one.

"You don't even share my dream. How could you even bring it up?"

"I'm not sure you have a dream, if you're purposely going to go somewhere where you know it'll be squashed. Who took on Rome, Francis? The saint you're named after? I've been reading your books about him ever since I got here. That's one reason I'll never call you Frankie. I love Saint Francis of Assisi. He changed the church, but at what cost? He died too young, disillusioned about what his order had become. And the Roman Catholic Church—just like all the rest of them in the world—stayed messy."

"He didn't 'take on' Rome. Emme, he held the Church up! Just like Pope Innocent dreamed."

"Until his shoulders drooped from the weight and he died."

"You don't understand what this means to me, X."

"I understand that you're a musician. I understand you're a former bad boy tryna find a way to make up for not just your own sins, but the sins of your father. Mother Nicole doesn't think you have a vocation to be a priest. She thinks you're confused."

"And what do you think, X?"

"I think you're afraid. You're at war with yourself because you want to be who you are, and you aren't quite sure if it's okay to do that. I understand it, because that's me, too. All day long."

"You *are* yourself."

"I'm a fragment of myself, Francis."

He gave me one of his ever-present heavy sighs and got quiet on me. Francis absently thumbed through the math book for a few minutes until finally he asked, "What are you trying to figure out here?"

He was talking about the math.

"I'm trying to figure out if you love me."

"We've known each other for three weeks, Emme."

"I know how I feel, even though it's only been three weeks."

He put his attention back on the math book. "Algebra? I'm great at algebra. Need help with that?"

"I love you, Francis."

"What are your weaknesses? That's what we need to pump up. And keep in mind that math is only one part of the test. If you're smart—and you are—you'll pass it. Go easy on the Ebonics during the English parts."

I turned back to the desk. "Apparently *you're* my weakness."

I'd taken a huge risk and told him how I felt about him. Now it was out there. I gave him a chance.

That was it for me. I determined that I wouldn't give him

the pleasure of seeing me cry. I'd have to pray that my feelings changed to become a God kind of love for him. Maybe I could be his Chiara, after all, one day. And maybe eventually it wouldn't hurt to know that we'd never be more than that.

Eventually.

We studied quietly for the next hour. He actually helped me get through the hardest part. At about eleven thirty he stood, stretched. I knew our night was over. That may have been the last long conversation I'd ever have with him. And he blew it.

I tossed out, "I'm leaving on my birthday."

"Fair enough. Where will you go?"

"I don't know yet. But I'll go without anyone being after me."

I got out of the chair. He took a step toward me, and I took one toward him. We faced each other, inching closer until we were close enough to kiss. I wondered what it would feel like to press my lips against his. My heart pounded at the thought of it. The thought gave me boldness and I flirted with him despite my earlier resolve. "I can't leave without you giving me a present."

I stood so close to him I could hear that his breathing had changed. His heart rate must have skyrocketed, like mine. He licked his lips and my stomach dropped to my feet.

"What would you like?"

"It ain't another pair of boots." I moved forward a little more. Now all he had to do was lower his mouth to mine.

His hands went to my hair. He slid my ponytail holder off with one hand, while the other tangled into my soft mane.

"Are you going to ask me to tell you that I love you for your birthday, Chiara? Don't you know me well enough to know the answer to that already?"

"I'm not even going to go there," I said, putting my arms around his neck. "I asked for that already, and you dropped the ball. There's just one thing I want from you." I wanted to kiss him so badly that I could hardly stand it.

His hands moved from my hair to circle my waist. I could feel his heart thundering inside his chest. "What do you want, Emme?"

"Finish the kiss we almost had at the mall."

"Now, or on your birthday?"

Oh, so now he wanted to play. He knew I wanted that kiss *now.* But I could take whatever he could dish out.

At least I hoped so.

I slid my hands into his hair. Played in its silkiness. Then pulled back from him, a bit. "I want it on my birthday."

He closed the space between us. "Are you sure that wasn't just a thank-you hug at the mall?"

"Is that all it was to you?"

"You tell me, you started it."

"Finish it, and I'll tell you what it was."

And then I stepped away from him. "Good night, Francis. I've got a little more studying to do. Close the door behind you."

"That's cold-blooded, X."

"Or not."

He promptly left the room, with a smirk on his face.

Twenty-Nine

If I wanted to effectively banish Francis from my presence, that little tease-fest after we studied was a good way to do it. Francis hardly spoke to me for the next few days.

Good.

It didn't take Father Rivera to make me feel like a Delilah, now. I should have brought a pair a scissors and asked Francis if he wanted a little off the top. My mama did not raise a tease, and I felt genuinely ashamed of myself, which only served to remind me. I needed my mama. Not Mother Nicole. Not Kiki, but my own mama. I missed her so much it felt like a physical wound sometimes.

What would you tell me if you were here, Mama? Should I have said anything to him about how I feel? Was that weak, I need to know if this really is love? Or lust? What's natural and what's evil? I'm not sure I know.

I'd made a fool of myself. All up in that man's face. And he didn't say he loved me. Shoot. What did I know? Just because he made goo-goo eyes at me didn't mean nothing. A lot of brothas looked at me like that. Tried to touch me, too!

Maybe I wanted to belong to somebody so badly, I'd manufactured a connection with Francis that wasn't there.

Shoot. I wouldn't make that mistake again.

I didn't know about Francis, but at least my guilt served me. Over and over again I asked God to forgive me for flirting like that. I put the GED books aside and focused wholly on prayer and the Gospels in preparation for the exorcism, which would take place at Jamilla's home that evening. The four of us, and the two other men from the team—the psychiatrist, Dr. Michael Black, and the family practitioner, Dr. Stormie Jaynes—had done their final examinations and deemed Jamilla beyond the reach of medical and psychiatric care. In other words, she needed an exorcist.

I was preparing for the night's activity by sitting in silence before the Lord after Vespers, when Francis knocked on the door. I told him to come in.

I wondered if he remembered that the last time he came in here, we almost ended up locking lips. He didn't let on if he did.

"Can we talk, Chiara?"

"Sure. Have a seat."

I got up from the chair and sat on the bed. He took my place at the desk.

He went totally didactic on me. "Okay, capsule course in exorcism. What was all the praying for?"

"Because exorcism is essentially a prayer ministry. And we fast to deny ourselves food, so we can hear His directions more clearly. When we are empty, God can fill us."

"Good girl. Who's the exorcist?"

I sighed. He'd gone over this stuff with me for weeks before we almost kissed. "Father Rivera is the exorcist, though everyone on the team is important."

"And how do we best offer service?"

"When we listen to Father Rivera and follow his directions. I have to do whatever he asks, no matter how crazy or mean it sounds. And I can't take any initiative, no matter how badly I want to."

"Who can you talk to during the rite?"

"We aren't supposed to have conversations during the rite. We're praying and watching. We can have a limited amount of sharing during breaks."

"Who are you forbidden to talk to?"

"Under no circumstances am I to speak to the possessed person or the demonic spirit."

"What if it says something foul to you?"

I folded my arms. "You don't trust me, do you?"

He showed that same bratty impatience he often does. "Come on, X! Cooperate. I just want to make sure you're ready. If I didn't trust you, do you think you'd be here? I put my butt on the line for you. Now work with me."

I glared at him. Finally unfolded my arms. "Fine. What else?"

"You didn't answer the last one."

I sighed again. In an exaggerated way. "If it says something foul, it's to throw me off my game. They don't want me to pray. They don't want Jamilla delivered, and they don't want to leave. They'll say whatever they can to stop us, including the vilest insults."

"And . . ."

"They know our weaknesses. Our sins. And they use them all as weapons against us."

He must have caught the bored tone in my voice.

"That's *real*, Emme. If you think that attack we got when you were exercising was deep, it was child's play compared to what they do during an exorcism. They can dredge up your worst secrets and blurt them out to everybody."

"I know that."

"Emme, I want to ask you to forgive me. You said I was always a gentleman with you, but we both know that's not true."

"I forgive you. If you'll forgive me for not being ladylike."

I would have told him that I didn't want the birthday kiss at all now. Mostly. But I ain't want that madness on our minds any more that it had to be. I ain't want the demons to have any fuel to use against us. At least none that I gave them.

He took a deep breath. Slapped his palms to his thighs. "All rightie, then. Last things. The icky stuff Mother Nicole warned you about."

"She said that I had to have a strong stomach. I can't react to the sight of blood, urine, excrement, vomit, or copious amounts of drool."

"That's my girl!"

I smiled at that despite myself. "Anything else, Professor?"

"I want to reiterate, X, you're going in there as the enemy to the Kingdom of darkness. Nothing we say can fully prepare you for what you're going to experience. This is a particularly bad case. And we're sure she has devils, not just demons. Very powerful beings. They ain't playin' around. Not these. Every bit of prayer we had these past few weeks was necessary and then some."

I looked in his eyes and saw a little fear there. "Are you nervous?"

"I don't think we could pray more than we did."

"We probably could have. Who prays enough?"

"Do you know if Kiki ever got things twisted? Could she be wrong about Jamilla dying if you aren't in there today?"

"We all get things twisted, sometimes. This isn't like Old Testament times, when people could kill you if you said a false prophetic word. I mean, it sucks to miss God like that, but the fact is, we're all seeing through a glass darkly, like 1 Corinthians 13:12 says."

He nodded, somber-looking. "True dat."

"But listen. The dreams your father and me had? And the state ID, which he totally checked out according to Mother Nicole? All of it is a bit too bizarre to be a mere coincidence."

"I know. That's what scares me the most."

"I think that's what should make us the most hopeful. God did all that so we could pray for Jamilla. And we've been praying. For Jamilla. For Father Rivera. For the team." I scooted closer to his chair, but didn't dare touch him. Didn't even hold his hand. We needed all our focus to be on the rite of exorcism. It was my first official one, and I wanted to be on my toes.

"We're all going to make it, Francis. I truly believe that."

"I hope you're right."

I didn't say anything, but I thought to myself, *Me, too.*

I prayed all the way to Jamilla's house. I didn't want to mess up anything or fool around and miss God. Already the day had been full of mishaps. Somebody kept calling the house and hanging up. I felt as snappy as I would if I had PMS. I lost the paperwork I needed to take with me to my GED test. Thoughts that my so-called gift of seeing into the spirit world wouldn't show buffeted me constantly. And my birthday was comin' up soon. The day of freedom.

On the way to the Jacobses' house, Father Rivera rode in the back of the car with me. I didn't want to sit up front with Francis. Neither of us needed the distraction of our mutual attraction. Nobody made small talk. Mother Nicole murmured the Jesus prayer while using some kind of crochet tool to make knotted prayer ropes out of wool yarn for the Orthodox monastic order she belonged to. It was a concrete reminder to me that her time at All Souls was as transitory as mine.

We arrived at Jamilla's simple house in the projects. Dr. Jaynes and Dr. Black were waiting for us outside. Michael Black was smoking a cigarette.

I winced at that. I thought the whole idea was to ditch your sins before we got there. But wasn't it a sin for me to judge? I repented for my wayward thought.

We got out of the car and greeted the men. I liked them both. Dr. Stormie Jaynes was a tall, African-American man in his fifties. He beat both me and Francis in the height. At 6'5", he seemed perpetually stooped from having to spend most of his time with shorter people.

Dr. Black was white, with wavy brown hair and an air of impatience. Like he was always thinking too far ahead, and you had to hustle to keep up with him. He was the psychiatrist. I wondered if his patients found him a sympathetic listener with his hurried manner.

We went to the door together, Father Rivera and Francis taking the lead. Mama Jacobs answered the door. She swept us into her concern as soon as she ushered us into the house.

The vibe in there was creepy, and not because we were in the hood. Even more creepy than when I had been there a few weeks ago.

I watched Francis for his reaction, and I could tell he felt it, too. Prayer connected us when we met. After the prayer marathons we'd participated in, it seemed we could pick up on a lot of what the others felt. At least where spiritual matters were concerned.

A quick scan of the room told me they'd prepared the living room exactly as Father Miguel had specified. The windows had been boarded on the inside. Anything can happen during an exorcism, including objects, and/or assistants, flying across the room. Demons love throwing people out of glass. I could attest to that after seeing Francis nearly hurled out of a glass door at Walgreens.

The room had been emptied of anything that could hurt someone. They'd moved the furniture out and placed a twin bed in the center of the room. A small, cheap plastic table was near it, with the required crucifix, prayer book, holy water, and blessed candle on it. Someone had placed a small holy card with the image of St. Francis of Assisi on it. I didn't know who in the family the saint meant a lot to, but I knew the picture would encourage Francis. I considered that a little gift of grace and evidence that God would be kind to us in the outcome.

At least I prayed He would.

Father Rivera donned his long black cassock with a purple stole draped across it. He looked every bit the kind of exorcist you'd see in a movie—still handsome, even though ill and in his older years.

He and I had finally found some measure of peace, and I was glad about that. I felt I owed it to him to be useful, and I didn't want to be present just to pray, although that was important. I wanted to use what they thought of as my "gift" to make a difference. What else was it for if not that?

The last few weeks had grown me. I didn't want to be the uneducated, smack-talkin' hoodrat anymore. I wanted to be a woman of God.

In Prada diva boots.

Jamilla's parents looked like they hadn't slept well for weeks. I knew Mama Jacobs and Pop literally had been through hell with Jamilla. I knew they wanted their nightmare to end.

Francis didn't need to make introductions, since her parents had already met the rest of the team. Mama Jacobs asked us if she could get us anything before we began. My mouth was so dry, my throat so parched that I kept swallowing. Nerves.

Father Rivera declined any drinks for us. No matter. There was a sense of urgency in the air, and we needed to get down to business. I'd consider it a fast from water for now and pray that God would bless my efforts.

Pop said to me, "Emme, we're countin' on you." Tears misted his eyes. "My little girl is not herself right now."

"It's okay, Mr. Jacobs. I understand."

"I want you to be prepared for what you're going to see."

"I saw her a couple of weeks ago."

He took a deep breath as though he was going to say more, then thought better of it and shook his head.

His words haunted me. *Prepared for what I'd see?* Weren't those the exact words the orderly used right before he opened the door to my mother's room?

I didn't need the hitch in my breathing to tell me I shouldn't think about my mother right now. I rocked back on my heels.

Now is not the time, X. You're here on a holy mission. This ain't about you, sistah.

But his words had watered a seed that had been planted long ago.

He walked Jamilla out of her room. Settled her in the center of the bed. She seemed less responsive now. It looked like you could move her body parts any way you wanted to, and she'd let you, not complaining, no matter how awkward the posture.

Father Miguel didn't waste any time getting started. With the crucifix, he made the sign of the cross in the name of the Father, the Son, and the Holy Spirit.

Jamilla's body stiffened, like she'd turned into a rod. She became a straight line. Her skin looked stretched, so that the natural lines and planes of her face were distorted. If you've ever seen someone who's had too many face-lifts, that's what she looked like. Only her entire body was pulled taut.

Father Rivera only reacted by praying the words Mother Nicole often prayed: "Lord, have mercy." Everyone repeated the prayer—except me. I'd gotten distracted while staring at Jamilla. I joined with the others after he said, "Christ, have mercy." We used plain speech, rather than chanted. It made it easier for us to focus, so we wouldn't be distracted by our efforts to sound right.

Francis told me it took about twenty minutes to get through the entire Roman ritual, which Father Rivera would repeat as many times as necessary. It could go hours, or even days. Some exorcisms took months. He said unless the exorcism was grueling, his father rarely took breaks during the process.

Next, Father Miguel began the Litany of Saints. This is when he called on the heavenly prayer warriors to intercede. Just like Francis said, he asked Jesus' mama for help.

"Holy Mary, pray for us. Holy Mother of God."

And we repeated, "Pray for us," after each name. It was uncomfortable for me. Even though Francis had told me this wasn't worshipping the saints and that it was no different than asking a live person to pray for me; still, I was Protestant through and through, and it felt weird. I was a little concerned my discomfort would affect Father Rivera's tasks. I went along with it, praying inwardly that these prayers we asked the saints for were okay.

A sound came rumbling out of Jamilla's stiff body like a cat purring. And it was loud! I could almost feel a vibration from it.

Every name Father Rivera called seemed to agitate Jamilla more, though she didn't move any part of her body. It was the rumbles that changed, becoming more and more beastly and ferocious sounding.

Father Rivera went through the names of holy angels, archangels, and saints I'd heard of, like the holy apostles and Saint Francis. Then he got to callin' on folks I'd never heard of, like Cosmas and Gervase and Protase. They sounded like something from a science class.

Science class? What in the world! We were in the middle of an exorcism I'd taken weeks to prepare for, and I was thinking crazy thoughts. My patience seemed to disappear, and I wondered if it was going to take forever to get through all those names. Finally, he got to the holy virgins and widows, and we were done.

With that part.

All kinds of strange thoughts began to invade my mind. I

wanted to go shopping. I thought about Kiki. I wondered if I should buy new makeup. It was weird, because I was really trying to concentrate. I wanted to laugh at the sounds Jamilla was making. I couldn't control the monkey chatter in my brain. Finally, Father Rivera, in a voice full of authority, spoke: "From all evil, deliver us, O Lord."

It was like something snapped in me. My mind was clear again, I immediately joined the prayers of deliverance.

Father Rivera spoke, "From all sin."

And we said, "Deliver us, O Lord."

"From your wrath."

"Deliver us, O Lord."

"From sudden and unprovided death."

That one got a loud, "Deliver us, O Lord," from me. I didn't want anything bad to happen in that room. To myself, I prayed another prayer for Father Rivera. And one for Jamilla.

Suddenly, Jamilla came alive. She screamed, "Help me!" In those two words, she sounded like my girl again.

I thought of Mama. Where was she? I didn't mean what hospital was she in. I meant where was the part of her that was her? Behind the voices and the weird postures. Whether it was schizophrenia, like they said, or something more sinister, did she ever push through the madness and beg somebody—*anybody*—for help?

I was lost again. Everyone was repeating, "We beg you to hear us."

I'd missed a whole section of the ritual. I tried to listen, but I couldn't stop thinking about Mama. I kept my eyes fixed on Jamilla. She seemed to be writhing in pain now. Moaning as if she were dying.

Then she stopped. She wasn't stiff anymore. It was as if she were perfectly normal. She sat up on the bed and spoke to Father Rivera. "You're sick. I can tell. You're in a lot of pain, and you're weak. Why don't we stop this? It's too much."

But her eyes looked wild and crazy. It was disconcerting to hear her say that so calmly, and yet her Charles Manson eyes challenged him.

Father Rivera spoke directly to the demon. "Jesus Christ paid the price on Calvary."

Then Father Rivera let out a painful cry.

Nobody moved. Mother Nicole softly chanted, "*Kyrie elieson, Christe elieson, Kyrie elieson, Christe elieson.* Lord, have mercy, Christ have mercy, Lord, have mercy, Christ have mercy."

Father Rivera seemed to be in agony. It took me a moment to realize what was happening: The demon was tormenting him by increasing the gnawing, cancerous pain.

Sweat beaded on Father Rivera's forehead, while the demon in Jamilla laughed hysterically. I wanted to scream at it to stop, but everyone had joined Mother Nicole in prayer.

I remembered the rules. I couldn't say anything to the demon. I was to do as I was directed, but it looked like Father Rivera was dying before us all.

A voice came out of Jamilla shouting cusswords. Father Rivera seemed to recover some of his strength. He touched the crucifix to Jamilla's head. At that she went wild. Every limb attacked him.

Francis, Stormie, and Mike sprang into action, grabbing the girl. Francis pinned her ankles, and the two doctors tried to keep her arms down. She had strength that wasn't hers, making their attempts to keep her safe a struggle for all of them.

Then Father Rivera went *off*! "I command you, unclean spirit and all your minions, by the mysteries of the incarnation, the passion, the resurrection, and the ascension of the Lord, Jesus Christ . . ."

A torrent of curses flew out of Jamilla's mouth. I mean, I've seen some R-rated movies. I've watched a few episodes of Def Comedy Jam, back in the day. I'd lived in the streets and met all kinds of foul people, but lemme tell you. Don't nuthin' cuss like a demon.

I thought the wallpaper would peel off!

It was as if that devil could hear my thoughts. Or maybe it just went there because I was the only person in the room who was new to the party.

Jamilla turned her head to me and called me everything but a child of God.

Why they always have to cuss me out?

But I wouldn't let that keep me from praying. I guess that made the devils in her even madder, because she let loose one of those *Exorcist* movie projectiles; and the next thing I knew, demon slime shot like a bullet at me and landed right on my diva boots.

Aw shoot! My eyes widened. *Oh no that heifer didn't!*

I was not feeling prayerful anymore. I wanted to strangle Milla, that demon, or whatever it was that chucked on my Pradas!

Father Rivera laid hands on Jamilla's forehead, saying, "They shall lay their hands on the sick and all will be well with them."

That girl jumped up, despite those three men holding her. Father Miguel did not remove his hand from her forehead, but now he sounded as if touching *her* were burning him.

I started praying again, for his sake, but I moved out of spitting range.

Jamilla's demon shouted, "You can't run from me." And called me out of my name again. I stood behind Francis. Let him get cussed out and spit on. He was the reason I was in this mess in the first place. And Jamilla was the second. But the real Milla wasn't nowhere near this place.

I'm telling you, that devil had some kind of Emme's boots radar. She hurled another slimy wad and yo, although Francis is 6'2" and standing at the foot of the bed, that demon spittle arched over his head and landed right on my boots.

Dang!

I started thinking. Okay, Lord, I ain't cut out for this kind of work. You gon' have to do something, because I'm wanting to whup her unholy behind.

God spoke, reminding me, *It's not Jamilla.*

That made me chill out. I kept praying, moving again to the opposite side of the room, all the way in the corner. I mean, it didn't matter if I wasn't standing by everybody else. God could hear my prayers wherever I was in the house.

Father Rivera let go of Jamilla, and she seemed to calm down. But the men stayed put and continued to hold her. It seemed to be a respite for everybody, 'cause girlfriend had gone buck wild before, and everybody needed a breather.

Father Rivera spoke the prayers softer now, his voice hypnotic, as he went through the Gospels. His lilting voice made the gospel of Luke come alive: "I was watching Satan fall like lightning that flashes from heaven. But mind: it is I that have given you the power to tread upon serpents and scorpions, and break the dominion of the enemy everywhere; nothing at all can injure you."

Amen, I said silently.

He recited the story in Luke 11 where Jesus drove out demons. It was like a mini Bible study right in the middle of the exorcism. We all continued to pray as he went through the passages—all from memory.

I started thinking Father Rivera was the bomb. And I prayed that he would forgive himself for falling in love and making a beautiful person like Francis. I also prayed that he and Francis would love each other in a way that was meaningful to both of them—before it was too late.

Just when I thought all was calm, all was bright, and Jamilla lay there mute and still, Father Rivera busted out with, "I cast you out, unclean spirit, along with every satanic power of the enemy."

What did he do that for? It was on. Again!

Jamilla lifted off the bed. When I say she lifted, I mean she went airborne. Sistah-girl levitated! She didn't float up like a slow-moving cloud. She shot up like a rocket. Those three big and tall men held her like she was a human canopy, and a symphony of the most unholy sounds imaginable poured out of her.

Father Rivera rolled with it. He picked up the holy water and started splashing it around on her and everybody else.

"Be gone and stay far from this creature of God, devils, for it is He who commands you, He who flung you headlong from the heights of heaven into the depths of hell."

The devil had a bad reaction to that one. It flung Jamilla down on that bed like God flung Lucifer out of heaven.

Blam!

The mouths on those things! They started in on everybody in

the room. And it was *bad.* Put Father Rivera's business all in the streets. I felt so sorry that Francis had to hear that thing talkin' smack about his mama.

But they didn't stop there. They attacked Francis.

I can't begin to repeat what they said. But it involved him and me and doing stuff even married folk ain't grown enough to do. I started thinking, *Yo, I'm too young for this. Father Rivera had the right idea. I don't need to hear all this.* I wondered what in the heck was wrong with Francis. Nobody under fifty should be exposed to the filth they were saying.

I stood there, my mouth wide open, because this was gettin' real personal. The next thing you know, Jamilla turned to me and hurled another wad.

I moved!

It moved! And landed right on my boots!

"Jesus, have mercy!" I yelled. They probably thought I was praying for Jamilla, but I was asking for some slack on my boots! I'd prayed for weeks for Jamilla. I was the one who needed some help now!

Father Rivera again commanded them to come out. "I adjure you, every unclean spirit, every specter from hell, every satanic power, in the name of Jesus Christ of Nazareth, who was led into the desert after His baptism from John to vanquish you in your citadel, come out now!"

Jamilla began to cough. I stepped waaaaay over to the side in case she started spittin' again. The room got colder. I could tell everyone in there felt it, too. And when I say cold, I mean see-your-breath cold. Wind that wasn't in the room started blowing. Jamilla coughed again, and I could see the form of a man in her face. The form of Asa.

Dang. That was crazy.

"Emme!" Father Rivera yelled.

Somehow I knew without him telling me he wanted to know what I saw. "It's a man's face on top of hers."

"Name yourself, demon!"

The face growled the word, "Deception." You could hear the sound of it all over the room, like that junk was in surround sound. It didn't come from Jamilla.

"What else do you see?"

"That's it."

Finally it stopped. Jamilla's body sprang up to a seated position; and in a high-pitched male voice, she began to speak. To me. "I know you. You are the daughter of Abigail. She belongs to us. She gave herself to us so that we would not take you."

"Silence!" Father Rivera shouted.

My knees began to tremble. Is that what happened to my mama? She was tryna spare me possession? Did she make some kind of pact with the devil? For me? It felt like my heart would burst, it pounded so violently. The presence of evil permeated the room. A crazy deep sense of suicidal despair swept through me. I dropped to my knees. My breath came in gasps. I didn't seem to be getting enough air. Something was asphyxiating me. I pulled at my throat. The thing in Jamilla laughed. Father Rivera prayed fervently.

"Go to her Francesco," he yelled.

In a flash, Francis was at my side.

I couldn't speak. Francis said in a panicked voice, "I feel something! It's right around her." Father Rivera turned his attention away from Jamilla to rebuke the force that had attacked me.

At that moment the presence begin to materialize. It was like a big, gray leech lying across my neck. Its razor teeth had sunk into my throat, cutting off my air.

"Release her," Father Rivera said, "you accursed, into everlasting fire!"

But it wouldn't leave.

"Fight it, Emme. Fight it."

Father Rivera's voice cut like a light through the dark despair I'd plunged into. But I couldn't speak. How could I cast it away from me?

Again, I heard his voice: "Fight!"

I began to focus my thoughts on God. On Mary, Jesus' mama. Francis said that in order to receive Christ, she had to empty herself and be totally available to the Holy Spirit. A demon was trying to kill me, but I didn't have to let it in. Especially if I was filled with the Holy Spirit.

I gave myself wholly to God. The only way I could make this devil flee was to resist him, by clinging to Christ.

Francis's and Father Rivera's prayers surrounded me. I could her Mother Nicole's, Mike's, and Stormie's. All of them prayed until my throat was loosed and the demon fell off me. When it fell, I saw it hit the floor. And it turned into a necklace. Yellow, with red beads and cowrie shells.

Father Rivera asked, "What's going on?"

"I saw a necklace. Then *poof*! it disappeared. It was a yellow-and-red beaded African-looking necklace with a cowrie shell charm."

The devil in Jamilla shouted, "NOOOOOOOOOOO!"

Now the devil changed tactics. Suddenly my thoughts were filled with my mother. When she first started hearing voices.

When she first told me how she could see demons, too. Her fear became mine in that moment. I could feel her anguish in every part of my soul.

"Fight it," Father Rivera yelled.

In my mind, I was plunged back into that hospital corridor, walking up to room number 379 B. The door flew open in my mind, and there she was.

I fixed my eyes on Jamilla at that moment and watched her face contort, until I was looking at my mother.

God help me.

I wanted to scream, but nothing emerged, until I heard a voice come out of Jamilla. "She is ours because of you." The exact words that had come out of my mother three years ago.

Father Rivera yelled, "Emme, what do you see?"

I was mute.

"What do you see?"

"My mother."

I rocked back on my heels. I had an overwhelming impulse to hurt myself. To throw myself out of the boarded window or tear at the skin on my face.

"Lying spirit," he said to Jamilla, "come out of this child, in the name of Jesus Christ."

The feelings were so strong that I balled my fist to keep them from clawing me. My fingernails bit into my palm.

Jamilla slumped forward, as if she were exhausted. Her head rolled on her neck like she had no muscle strength. With her head to one side, she whispered, "Please."

Mama Jacobs cried out, "That's my baby! That's her voice."

It was in that moment that I realized why Francis did this

work. Why everybody on the team did it. That little, single word, *please,* held so much terror. I had only experienced a portion of the evil that visited my girl. She lived with it every day. Tormenting her. Forcing her to harm herself. And all she could do in her weariness, this one tiny soul, was plead with us with that one word.

One more command from Father Rivera. One screeching shriek of terror out of Jamilla. She opened her mouth wide. Unnaturally wide, as if something were stretching it beyond its capacity.

Father Rivera yelled, "Emme!"

I watched as a serpent slithered out of her mouth.

"It's a serpent. It's beautiful. Full of light, but it has arms and legs." I watched it move through the ceiling, leaving a gray stain.

Jamilla fell onto the bed, as if she were dead.

"It went upstairs," I said.

Father Rivera said, "We must go upstairs." He ordered her parents to hold her. And the team bounded upstairs. I directed the team to the demon that hovered around a cheap, cardboard musical jewelry box. It had a lid that when you opened it, a ballerina danced. Jamilla had had it since she was a kid. She kept her few treasures in that box. And the demon dove inside like he was . . .

A necklace.

The parents had cleaned the house of all traces of Santeria that Jamilla had told them about—but she had held on to that one thing.

Because it was from him. Because he kissed her. Because his seductive power lured her in. And because she thought he was a god.

I didn't go near the box.

"It's in her jewelry box," I said. "I think it's one of those necklaces dedicated to the Orishas. He probably gave it to her, and she thought it was a love token or something."

Francis spoke: "If she kept it, it would have infected her again."

"It would have killed her," I said. "It would have had help."

Francis quoted the Scripture: "When an unclean spirit goes out of someone it wanders through waterless country looking for a place to rest, and not finding one it says, 'I will go back to the home I came from.' But on arrival, finding it swept and tidied, it then goes off and brings seven other spirits more wicked than itself, and they go in and set up house there, and so that person ends up worse than before."

Like they say at Father Rivera's church, the Word of the Lord. God had spoken.

Thirty

I rode home barefoot. I couldn't hang with the diva boots, now that they had devil slime all over them. Tossed those babies at the Jacobses' house.

Nobody talked on the way home, but Father Rivera did say one thing to me. "You did good."

Lord, have mercy.

I don't know what the rest of them were feeling, but a residual melancholy clung to me. I couldn't shake it for days afterward. Not even when I went to take my GED exam, which should have been a happy occasion. Sometimes, I'd cry for no reason. Other times, I'd cry for Jamilla and what she'd suffered. I cried a lot for my mother, and I knew what I had to do.

Francis once told me that at every exorcism, you die a little. I didn't believe him at the time. I'd dealt with demons all my life. I thought I knew what was up with them; but my mother, and God only knows who else, protected me. I was shielded from knowing the depths of evil the way Jamilla had experienced it.

I couldn't stop thinking about what the demon said about my mother, "She's ours because of you."

I know liars lie, but they also add a little bit of truth to the mix. I couldn't trust a demon. That's why I didn't want to talk to them. But one did speak. The words "Because of you" churned over and over in my soul.

I remember when I used to believe that happily ever after was as final as heaven. I guess I needed to hold on to that kind of hope, just so I could go on. But a hard-knock life taught a sistah that what you think is happily ever after has a shadowy side, especially when you've been touched by evil.

I went to see Jamilla two days after her exorcism. The house was full of happiness and peace now, but a vein of sorrow, barely susceptible, ran through the Jacobs family, and I knew from experience it wasn't goin' nowhere.

Mama Jacobs invited me in, wiping her hands on an apron. The house smelled of cooked roast, collard greens, rice, and yams. Jamilla's daddy had taken off a few days from work. He prowled around the house like a tiger, as though circling his little cub would protect her from further spiritual ills.

I found Jamilla in the living room on that rent-to-own couch with the big, crazy flowers. She looked like Jamilla again. Mostly. It would take time for her body to heal from the abuse it had suffered.

She got up and came and hugged me. "Hey, girl." Then her eyes swept to the floor like she was ashamed. "Thanks."

"It's all good."

We sat down and didn't even talk about it. The exorcism team had already given her instruction. Sistah had to be diligent now. She'd have to watch and pray and stay in that

Word of God like it would save her life. It had. And it would.

She told me how happy she was that she'd be able to go back to school. She told me what was up with people we use to hang with. And then we talked about the fly gear I had.

"W'sup with you and Frank, girl? I could tell he was diggin' you, even when I was possessed!"

"We're just cool, Milla. He's on a mission. It's a God thing. I'm gon' let that brotha do his thing."

"Girl, are you crazy?"

"Naw. Just real, Jamilla. The brotha's don't save you. God can use them to bless you, but He's the only one who can save you. I can't afford to get that twisted." I looked her right in her eyes. "You can't either, sis. Not even if a brotha comes to you lookin' like an angel of light."

I spent the night with her. We ate buttery popcorn, watched silly movies from our childhood, and let ourselves be a couple a lil' girls again.

We hugged good-bye, puttin' more into that hug than we could say. "Happy Birthday, Em," Jamilla said. "I'll get you a gift. I promise."

I looked at her square. "You already have."

On my birthday I got up early, dressed, and packed my clothes in a duffel bag. I walked around Francis's room, touching his things. His Bibles. His books. Even the creepy books about demons and exorcism. He'd left one of his guitars, an electric one, in the closet. I touched that too, and imagined him playing his Monk Funk once he became a priest.

I love him, I thought.

Maybe I was wrong about everything. Maybe he was meant to be a Catholic priest, and I wanted him for myself, and couldn't see what God was doing in his life.

Almost as if on cue, I heard a knock at the door. There stood Francis, hoding a big box wrapped in Happy Birthday paper and tied with a huge red bow. "For the birthday girl. Or should I say, the birthday grown woman."

"You crazy man! You didn't have to give me a present."

He gave me a little shrug. "It's not what you asked for . . ."

I didn't go there with him.

I took the box out of his hands and sat on the bed to open it. He watched, grinnin' like a fool, leaning up against the doorjamb.

He'd wrapped it so I didn't have to bother tearing through paper and tape. I lifted the lid. Inside were a pair of Prada boots. Different from the others. Better, actually.

I cracked up. Got up from the bed to go hug him. I felt so happy and silly that I'd forgotten how combustible the two of us could be.

I wrapped my arms around him and heard him catch his breath as my face moved toward his. I didn't see a "Don't kiss me" expression on his face. It was more like, "Aw, man. You caught me off guard again." We froze in place, me in his arms.

Francis rubbed his cheek against mine, "Stay, Emme."

I squeezed him. "I can't, Francis."

"Please stay with me," he whispered in my ear.

I held him for a long time. Those were the words I longed to hear. Words I'd waited for. Hoped for. I didn't have to hide from the foster care system now. His father had come to accept me. I was even part of the team, even though I still felt useless.

I backed away from him. "Why should I stay, Francis?"

"Because I need you."

"What about God? The priesthood? Aren't you needed there?"

He looked away. "I don't know."

"You want me to stay and you don't know what you're going to do?"

"I'll work through it."

I picked up my duffel bag. Slung it over one shoulder. Picked up the box of boots and tucked them under my arm. "Walk me out."

"X, don't leave."

"Francis, I know you're conflicted. Unsure. Welcome to my life. I'm leaving here with money your father slipped me to enter a world where I don't know what's going to happen. I only know I need to get to my mama. I need to get her help, no matter what is ailing her. I'm sure about that much. But you're not sure about me, Francis. So I'ma let you work through that on yo' own."

I walked out the bedroom with him trailing behind me. "I am sure about you, and I'd rather work it out with you around me. I asked you to stay, X. Do you know how hard that was for me to ask?"

I swung around to face him. "Yes, I do, Francis. And that's the problem. It shouldn't have been that hard."

He didn't say anything.

"On second thought, don't walk me out."

"I'll take you to the bus station."

"I'll catch a city bus." I took a deep breath. "I can't do this with you, Francis. I just can't. Okay?"

He nodded.

" 'Bye, Francis." I turned to walk away, but I had to say one more thing to him. From my heart. I faced him again. "Francis."

"What is it, X?"

"The Lord bless you and keep you; the Lord show His face to you, and have mercy on you; the Lord turn His countenance to you, and give you peace. The Lord bless you."

"The blessing of Saint Francis. You think of everything."

"It's a gift," I said, and was rewarded with that single, maddening, irresistible dimple.

But I had to resist his charm. I had to go get my mama.

I walked to the door. I couldn't look behind me. As I turned the knob, Francis grabbed my wrist. He pulled me into an embrace. Those golden-flecked eyes of his bored into mine, and he lowered his head and kissed me.

Every other kiss from men in dark corners forcing themselves on me all disappeared. All of those memories receded in the sweetness of his mouth. This was my first kiss. This was my only kiss. This was the prince awakening the princess so she could live again.

Tears streamed down my cheeks, but I kissed him until I felt his tears mingle with mine. Finally, he released me.

He choked out the words, "Happy Birthday, Exorsistah. I love you very much."

All the words were gone from me. I couldn't say good-bye to him again. I just wanted to go with his love all over me.

He loved me!

He really did. I could feel it.

I wiped my face, tucked the diva boots firmly under my arms, and walked out the door into my new life. All would be well.